Timothy Allen

EDWARD ST. AUBYN is the author of *A Clue to the Exit, On the Edge,* and the acclaimed Patrick Melrose novels (*Never Mind, Bad News, Some Hope,* and *Mother's Milk,* which was shortlisted for the Man Booker Prize). *At Last* is the final installment in the Melrose novels.

ALSO BY EDWARD ST. AUBYN

Mother's Milk

Some Hope

A Clue to the Exit

On the Edge

At Last

EDWARD ST. AUBYN

Picador

Farrar, Straus and Giroux

New York

AT LAST. Copyright © 2011 by Edward St. Aubyn. All rights reserved.
Printed in the United States of America. For information, address Picador,
175 Fifth Avenue, New York, N.Y. 10010.

www.picadorusa.com
www.twitter.com/picadorusa • www.facebook.com/picadorusa
picadorbookroom.tumblr.com

Picador® is a U.S. registered trademark and is used by Farrar, Straus and Giroux
under license from Pan Books Limited.

For book club information, please visit www.facebook.com/picadorbookclub
or e-mail marketing@picadorusa.com.

Grateful acknowledgement is made for permission to reprint excerpts from the following:
'Fly Me to the Moon (In Other Words)', words and music by Bart Howard. TRO –©–
Copyright 1954 (renewed) by Hampshire House Publishing Corp., New York, NY. Used
by permission.
'I Got Plenty o' Nuttin', words and music by George Gershwin, Du Bose Heyward and
Ira Gershwin. Copyright © 1935 (renewed) by Chappell & Co., Inc. (ASCAP). All rights
administered by Warner/Chappell North America Ltd.
Excerpt from 'Burnt Norton', Part I of *Four Quartets* by T. S. Eliot, copyright © 1936 by
Harcourt, Inc., and renewed © 1964 by T. S. Eliot, reprinted by permission of Houghton
Mifflin Harcourt Publishing Company.
'Dutch Graves in Bucks County' from *The Collected Poems of Wallace Stevens* by Wallace
Stevens, copyright © 1954 by Wallace Stevens and renewed © 1982 by Holly Stevens. Used
by permission of Alfred A. Knopf, a division of Random House, Inc.

The Library of Congress has cataloged the Farrar, Straus and Giroux edition as follows:

St. Aubyn, Edward, 1960–
    At last / Edward St. Aubyn. — 1st American ed.
    p. cm.
    ISBN 978-0-374-29889-0
    1. Psychological fiction.   2. Domestic fiction.   I. Title.

PR6069.T134 A93 2012
823'.914—dc23

2011034964

Picador ISBN 978-1-250-02390-2

Originally published in Great Britain by Picador, an imprint of Pan Macmillan

First published in the United States by Farrar, Straus and Giroux

First Picador Edition: January 2013

10 9 8 7 6 5 4 3 2 1

For Bo

At Last

1

'Surprised to see me?' said Nicholas Pratt, planting his walking stick on the crematorium carpet and fixing Patrick with a look of slightly aimless defiance, a habit no longer useful but too late to change. 'I've become rather a memorial-creeper. One's bound to at my age. It's no use sitting at home guffawing over the ignorant mistakes of juvenile obituarists, or giving in to the rather monotonous pleasure of counting the daily quota of extinct contemporaries. No! One has to "celebrate the life": there goes the school tart. They say he had a good war, but I know better! – that sort of thing, put the whole achievement in perspective. Mind you, I'm not saying it isn't all very moving. There's a sort of swelling orchestra effect to these last days. And plenty of horror, of course. Padding about on my daily rounds from hospital bed to memorial pew and back again, I'm reminded of those oil tankers that used to dash themselves onto the rocks every other week and the flocks of birds dying on the beaches with their wings stuck together and their bewildered yellow eyes blinking.'

Nicholas glanced into the room. 'Thinly attended,' he murmured, as if preparing a description for someone else. 'Are those people your mother's religious friends? Too extraordinary. What colour would you call that suit? Aubergine? *Aubergine à la crème d'oursin?* I must go to Huntsman and get one knocked up. What do you mean, you have no Aubergine? Everyone was wearing it at Eleanor Melrose's. Order a mile of it straight away!

'I suppose your aunt will be here soon. She'll be an all too familiar face amidst the Aubergines. I saw her last week in New York and I'm pleased to say I was the first to tell her the tragic news about your mother. She burst into tears and ordered a *croque monsieur* to swallow with her second helping of diet pills. I felt sorry for her and got her asked to dinner with the Blands. Do you know Freddie Bland? He's the smallest billionaire alive. His parents were practically dwarfs, like General and Mrs. Tom Thumb. They used to come into the room with a tremendous fanfare and then disappear under a console table. Baby Bland has taken to being serious, the way some people do in their senile twilight. She's decided to write a book about Cubism, of all ridiculous subjects. I think it's really part of her being a perfect wife. She knows what a state Freddie used to get into over her birthday, but thanks to her new hobby, all he has to do now is get Sotheby's to wrap up a revolting painting of a woman with a face like a slice of watermelon by that arch fake Picasso, and he knows she'll be over the moon. Do you know what Baby said to me? At breakfast, if you please, when I was almost defenceless.' Nicholas put on a simpering voice:

' "Those divine birds in late Braque are really just an excuse for the sky."

' "Such a good excuse," I said, choking on my first sip of coffee, "so much better than a lawn mower or a pair of clogs. It shows he was in complete control of his material."

'Serious, you see. It's a fate I shall resist with every last scrap of my intelligence, unless Herr Doktor Alzheimer takes over, in which case I'll have to write a book about Islamic art to show that the towel-heads have always been much more civilized than us, or a fat volume on how little we know about Shakespeare's mother and her top-secret Catholicism. Something serious.

'Anyhow, I'm afraid Aunt Nancy rather bombed with the Blands. It must be hard to be exclusively social and entirely friendless at the same time. Poor thing. But do you know what struck me, apart from Nancy's vibrant self-pity, which she had the nerve to pretend was grief? What struck me about those two girls, your mother and your aunt, was that they are, were – my life is spent wobbling between tenses – completely American. Their father's connection with the Highlands was, let's face it, entirely liquid and after your grandmother sacked him he was hardly ever around. He spent the war with those dimwits the Windsors in Nassau; Monte Carlo after the war; and finally foundered in the bar of White's. Of the tribe who are blind drunk every day of their lives from lunch until bedtime, he was by far the most charming, but frustrating I think as a father. At that level of drunkenness one's essentially trying to embrace a drowning man. The odd eruption of sentimentality for the twenty minutes the drink took him that way was no substitute for the steady flow of self-sacrificing kindness that has always inspired my own efforts as a father. With what I admit have been mixed results. As

I'm sure you know, Amanda hasn't spoken to me for the last fifteen years. I blame her psychoanalyst, filling her never very brilliant little head with Freudian ideas about her doting Papa.'

Nicholas's rotund style of delivery was fading into an increasingly urgent whisper, and the knuckles of his blue-veined hands were white from the effort of holding himself upright. 'Well, my dear, we'll have another little chat after the ceremony. It's been marvellous finding you on such good form. My condolences and all that, although if ever there was a "merciful release", it was in the case of your poor mother. I've become something of a Florence Nightingale in my old age, but even the Lady with the Lamp had to beat a retreat in the face of that terrifying ruin. It's bound to act as a brake on the rush to get me canonized but I prefer to pay visits to people who can still enjoy a bitchy remark and a glass of champagne.'

He seemed about to leave but then turned back. 'Try not to be bitter about the money. One or two friends of mine who've made a mess of that side of things have ended up dying in National Health wards and I must say I've been very impressed by the humanity of the mostly foreign staff. Mind you, what is there to do with money except spend it when you've got it or be bitter about it when you haven't? It's a very limited commodity in which people invest the most extraordinary emotions. What I suppose I really mean is *do* be bitter about the money; it's one of the few things it can do: siphon off some bitterness. Do-gooders have sometimes complained that I have too many bêtes noires, but I need my bêtes noires to get the noire out of me and into the bêtes. Besides, that side of your family has had a good run. What is it now? Six generations with every single descendant, not just the eldest son, essentially idle? They may have taken on the camouflage of work, especially in America, where everyone had to have an office, if only to swivel about with their shoes on the desk for half an hour before lunch, but there's been no necessity. It must be rather thrilling, although I can't speak from experience, for you and your children, after this long exemption from competition, to get stuck in. God knows what I would have made of my life if I hadn't divided my time between town and country, between home and abroad, between wives and mistresses. I have divided time and now doth time divide me, what? I must take a closer look at these religious fanatics your mother surrounded herself with.'

Nicholas hobbled off with no pretence that he expected any response other than silent fascination.

When Patrick looked back on the way that illness and dying had torn apart Eleanor's flimsy shamanic fantasies, Nicholas's 'religious fanatics' seemed to him more like credulous draft-dodgers. At the end of her life Eleanor had been thrown into a merciless crash-course in self-knowledge, with only a 'power animal' in one hand and a rattle in the other. She had been left with the steepest practice of all: no speech, no movement, no sex, no drugs, no travel, no spending, hardly any food; just alone in silent contemplation of her thoughts. If contemplation was the word. Perhaps she felt that her thoughts were contemplating her, like hungry predators.

'Were you thinking about her?' said a soft Irish voice. Annette rested a healing hand on Patrick's forearm and tilted her understanding head to one side.

'I was thinking that a life is just the history of what we give our attention to,' said Patrick. 'The rest is packaging.'

'Oh, I think that's too stark,' said Annette. 'Maya Angelou says that the meaning of our lives is the impact we have on other people, whether we make them feel good or not. Eleanor always made people feel good, it was one of her gifts to the world. Oh,' she added with sudden excitement, gripping Patrick's forearm, 'I only made this connection on the way in: we're in Mortlake crematorium to say farewell to Eleanor, and guess what I took to read to her on the last occasion I saw her? You'll never guess. *The Lady of the Lake*. It's an Arthurian whodunit, not very good actually. But that says it all, doesn't it? Lady of the lake – Mortlake. Given Eleanor's connection with water and her love of the Arthurian legends.'

Patrick was stunned by Annette's confidence in the consoling power of her words. He felt irritation being usurped by despair. To think that his mother had chosen to live among these resolute fools. What knowledge was she so determined to avoid?

'Who can say why a crematorium and a bad novel should have vaguely similar names?' said Patrick. 'It's tantalizing to be taken so far beyond the rational mind. I tell you who would be very receptive to that sort of connection: you see the old man over there with the walking stick. Do tell him. He loves that kind of thing. His name is Nick.' Patrick dimly remembered that Nicholas loathed this abbreviation.

'Seamus sends his best,' said Annette, accepting her dismissal cheerfully.

'Thank you.' Patrick bowed his head, trying not to lose control of his exaggerated deference.

What was he doing? It was all so out of date. The war with Seamus and his mother's Foundation was over. Now that he was an orphan everything was perfect. He seemed to have been waiting all his life for this sense of completeness. It was all very well for the Oliver Twists of this world, who started out in the enviable state it had taken him forty-five years to achieve, but the relative luxury of being brought up by Bumble and Fagin, rather than David and Eleanor Melrose, was bound to have a weakening effect on the personality. Patient endurance of potentially lethal influences had made Patrick the man he was today, living alone in a bedsit, only a year away from his latest visit to the Suicide Observation Room in the Depression Wing of the Priory Hospital. It had felt so ancestral to have delirium tremens, to bow down, after his disobedient youth as a junkie, to the shattering banality of alcohol. As a barrister he was reluctant nowadays to kill himself illegally. The alcohol felt deep, humming down the bloodline. He could still remember, when he was five, taking a donkey ride among the palm trees and the packed red-and-white flowerbeds of Monte Carlo's Casino Gardens, while his grandfather sat on a green bench shaking uncontrollably, clamped by sunlight, a stain spreading slowly through the pearl-grey trousers of his perfectly cut suit.

Lack of insurance forced Patrick to pay for his own stay in the Priory, exhausting all his funds in a thirty-day gamble on recovery. Unhelpfully short from a psychiatric point of view, a month was still long enough for him to become immediately infatuated with a twenty-year-old patient called Becky. She looked like Botticelli's Venus, improved by a bloody trellis of razor cuts crisscrossing its way up her slender white arms. When he first saw her in the lounge of the Depression Wing, her radiant unhappiness sent a flaming arrow into the powder keg of his frustration and emptiness.

'I'm a self-harming resistant depressive,' she told him. 'They've got me on eight different kinds of pills.'

'Eight,' said Patrick admiringly. He was down to three himself: the daytime antidepressant, the night-time antidepressant, and the thirty-two oxazepam tranquillizers a day he was taking to deal with the delirium tremens.

Insofar as he could think at all on such a high dose of oxazepam, he could think only of Becky. The next day, he heaved himself off his crackling mattress and slouched to the Depression Support Group in the hope of seeing her again. She was not there, but Patrick could not escape from joining the circle of tracksuited depressives. 'As to sports, let our wear do it for us,' he sighed, slumping down in the nearest chair.

An American called Gary kicked off the sharing with the words, 'Let me give you a scenario: suppose you were sent to Germany for work, and suppose a friend you hadn't heard from in a long time called you up and came to visit with you from the States . . .' After a tale of shocking exploitation and ingratitude, he asked the group what he should say to this friend. 'Cut them out of your life,' said the bitter and abrasive Terry, 'with friends like that, who needs enemies?'

'Okay,' said Gary, relishing his moment, 'and suppose I told you that this "friend" was my mother, what would you say then? Why would that be so different?'

Consternation raced through the Group. A man, who had been feeling 'completely euphoric' since his mother had come over on Sunday and taken him out to buy a new pair of trousers, said that Gary should never abandon his mother. On the other hand, there was a woman called Jill who had been 'for a long walk by the river I wasn't supposed to come back from – well, put it this way, I did come back *very wet*, and I said to Dr. Pagazzi, who I love to bits, that I thought it had something to do with my mother, and he said, "We're not even going to go there."' Jill said that, like her, Gary should have nothing to do with his mother. At the end of the session, the wise Scottish moderator tried to shield the group from this downpour of self-centred advice.

'Someone once asked me why mothers are so good at pushing our buttons,' he said, 'and the answer I gave was, "Because they put them there in the first place."'

Everyone nodded gloomily, and Patrick asked himself, not for the first time, but with renewed desperation, what it would mean to be free, to live beyond the tyranny of dependency and conditioning and resentment.

After the Support Group, he saw a caved-in, illicitly smoking, barefooted Becky go down the staircase beyond the laundry. He followed her and found her crumpled on the stairs, her giant pupils swimming in a pool of tears. 'I hate this place,' she said. 'They're going to throw me out because they say I've got a bad attitude. But I only stayed in bed because I'm so *depressed*. I don't know where I'm going to go, I can't face going back to my parents.'

She was screaming to be saved. Why not run away with her to the bedsit? She was one of the few people alive who was more suicidal than him. They could lie on the bed together, Priory refugees, one convulsing while the other slashed. Why not take her back and let her finish the job for him? Her bluest veins to bandage, her whitening lips to kiss. No no no no no. He was too well, or at least too old.

These days he could only remember Becky with deliberate effort. He often watched his obsessions pass over him like so many blushes, and by doing nothing about them, watched them fade. Becoming an orphan was a thermal on which this new sense of freedom might continue to rise, if only he had the courage not to feel guilty about the opportunity it presented.

Patrick drifted towards Nicholas and Annette, curious to see the outcome of his matchmaking.

'Stand by the graveside or the furnace,' he heard Nicholas instructing Annette, 'and repeat these words, "Goodbye, old thing. One of us was bound to die first and I'm delighted it was you!" That's my spiritual practice, and you're welcome to adopt it and put it into your hilarious "spiritual tool box".'

'Your friend is absolutely priceless,' said Annette, seeing Patrick approaching. 'What he doesn't realize is that we live in a loving universe. And it loves you too, Nick,' she assured Nicholas, resting her hand on his recoiling shoulder.

'I've quoted Bibesco before,' snapped Nicholas, 'and I'll quote him again: "To a man of the world, the universe is a suburb".'

'Oh, he's got an answer to everything, hasn't he?' said Annette. 'I expect he'll joke his way into heaven. St. Peter loves a witty man.'

'Does he?' said Nicholas, surprisingly appeased. 'That's the best thing I've heard yet about that bungling social secretary. As if the Supreme Being would consent to spend eternity surrounded by a lot of nuns and paupers and par-boiled missionaries, having his lovely concerts ruined by the rattle of spiritual tool boxes and the screams of the faithful, boasting about their crucifixions! What a relief that an enlightened command has finally reached the concierge at the Pearly Gates: "For Heaven's sake, send Me a conversationalist!"'

Annette looked at Nicholas with humorous reproach.

'Ah,' he said, nodding at Patrick, 'I never thought I'd be so grateful to see your impossible aunt.' He lifted his stick and waved it at Nancy. She stood in the doorway looking exhausted by her own haughtiness, as if her raised eyebrows might not be able to stand the strain much longer.

'Help!' she said to Nicholas. 'Who are these peculiar people?'

'Zealots, Moonies, witch-doctors, would-be terrorists, every variety of religious lunatic,' explained Nicholas, offering Nancy his arm. 'Avoid eye contact, stick close to me and you may live to tell the tale.'

Nancy flared up when she saw Patrick. 'Of all the days *not* to have the funeral,' she said.

'Why?' he asked, confused.

'It's Prince Charles's wedding. The only other people who might have come will be at Windsor.'

'I'm sure you'd be there as well, if you'd been

invited,' said Patrick. 'Don't hesitate to nip down with a Union Jack and a cardboard periscope if you think you'd find it more entertaining.'

'When I think how we were brought up,' wailed Nancy, 'it's too ridiculous to think what my sister did with . . .' She was lost for words.

'The golden address book,' purred Nicholas, gripping his walking stick more tightly as she sagged against him.

'Yes,' said Nancy, 'the golden address book.'

2

Nancy watched her infuriating nephew drift towards his mother's coffin. Patrick would never understand the fabulous way that she and Eleanor had been brought up. Eleanor had stupidly rebelled against it, whereas it had been ripped from Nancy's prayerfully clasped hands.

'The golden address book,' she sighed again, locking arms with Nicholas. 'I mean, for example, Mummy only ever had one car accident in her entire life, but even then, when she was hanging upside down in the buckled metal, she had the Infanta of Spain dangling next to her.'

'That's very in-depth, I must say,' said Nicholas. 'A car accident can get one tangled up with all sorts of obscure people. Picture the commotion at the College of Heralds if a drop of one's blood landed on the dashboard of a lorry and mingled with the bodily fluids of the brute whose head had been dashed against the steering wheel.'

'Do you always have to be so facetious?' snapped Nancy.

'I do my best,' said Nicholas. 'But you can't pretend that your mother was a fan of the common man. Didn't she buy the entire village street that ran along the boundary wall of the Pavillon Colombe, in order to demolish it and expand the garden? How many houses was that?'

'Twenty-seven,' said Nancy, cheering up. 'They weren't all demolished. Some of them were turned into exactly the right kind of ruin to go with the house. There were follies and grottos, and Mummy had a replica made of the main house, only fifty times smaller. We used to have tea there, it was like something out of *Alice in Wonderland*.' Nancy's face clouded over. 'There was a horrible old man who refused to sell, although Mummy offered him far too much for his poky little house, and so there was an inward bulge following the line of the old wall, if you see what I'm saying.'

'Every paradise demands a serpent,' said Nicholas.

'He did it just to annoy us,' said Nancy. 'He put a

French flag on the roof and used to play Edith Piaf all day long. We had to smother him in vegetation.'

'Maybe he liked Edith Piaf,' said Nicholas.

'Oh, don't be funny! Nobody could like Edith Piaf at that volume.'

Nicholas sounded sour to Nancy's sensitive ear. So what if Mummy hadn't wanted ordinary people pressing up against her property? It was hardly surprising when everything else was so divine. Fragonard had painted *Les Demoiselles Colombe* in that garden, hence the necessity for having Fragonards in the house. The original owners had hung a pair of big Guardis in the drawing room, hence the authenticity of getting them back.

Nancy couldn't help being haunted by the splendour and the wreckage of her mother's family. One day she was going to write a book about her mother and her aunts, the legendary Jonson Sisters. She had been collecting material for years, fascinating bits and pieces that just needed to be organized. Only last week, she had sacked a hopeless young researcher – the tenth in a succession of greedy egomaniacs who wanted to be paid in advance – but not before her latest slave had discovered a copy of her grandmother's birth certificate. According to this wonderfully quaint document, Nancy's grandmother had been 'Born in Indian Country'. How could the daughter of a young army officer, born at this unlikely address, have guessed, as she tottered about among the creaky pallet beds and restless horses of an adobe fort in the Western Territories, that her own daughters would be tottering along the corridors of European castles and filling their houses with the debris of failed dynasties – splashing about in Marie Antoinette's black marble bath, while their yellow Labradors dozed on carpets from the throne room of the imperial palace in Peking? Even the lead garden tubs on the terrace of the Pavillon Colombe had been made for Napoleon. Gold bees searching through silver blossoms, dripping in the rain. She always thought that Jean had made Mummy buy those tubs to take an obscure revenge on Napoleon for saying that his ancestor, the great duc de Valençay, was 'a piece of shit in a silk stocking'. What she liked to say was that Jean kept up the family tradition, minus the silk stocking. Nancy gripped Nicholas's arm even more tightly, as if her horrid stepfather might try to steal him as well.

If only Mummy hadn't divorced Daddy. They had such a glamorous life in Sunninghill Park, where she and Eleanor were brought up. The Prince of Wales used to drop in all the time, and there were never fewer than twenty people staying in the house, having the best fun ever. It was true that Daddy had the bad habit of buying Mummy extremely expensive presents, which she had to pay for. When she said, 'Oh, darling, you shouldn't have,' she really meant it. She grew nervous of commenting on the garden. If she said that a border needed a little more blue, a couple of days later she would find that Daddy had flown in some impossible flower from Tibet which bloomed for about three minutes and cost as much as a house. But before the drink took over, Daddy was handsome and warm and so infectiously funny that the food often arrived shaking at the table, because the footmen were laughing too much to hold the platters steadily.

When the Crash came, lawyers flew in from America to ask the Craigs to rack their brains for something they could do without. They thought and thought. They obviously couldn't sell Sunninghill Park. They had to go on entertaining their friends. It would be too cruel and too inconvenient to sack any of the servants. They couldn't do without the house in Bruton Street for overnight stays in London. They needed two Rolls-Royces and two chauffeurs because Daddy was incorrigibly punctual and Mummy was incorrigibly late. In the end they sacrificed one of the six news-papers that each guest received with their breakfast. The lawyers relented. The pools of Jonson money were too deep to pretend there was a crisis; they were not stock-market speculators, they were industrialists and owners of great blocks of urban America. People would always need hardened fats and dry-cleaning fluids and somewhere to live.

Even if Daddy had been too extravagant, Mummy's marriage to Jean was a folly that could be explained only by the resulting title – she was definitely jealous of Aunt Gerty being married to a grand duke. Jean's role in the Jonson story was to disgrace himself, as a liar and a thief, a lecherous stepfather and a tyranni-cal husband. While Mummy lay dying of cancer, Jean threw one of his tantrums, screaming that doubt was being cast on his honour by her will. She was leav-ing him her houses and paintings and furniture only for his lifetime and then on to her children, as if he couldn't be trusted to leave them to the children him-self. He knew perfectly well that they were Jonson possessions . . . and on and on; the morphine, the pain, the screaming, the indignant promises. She changed her will and Jean went back on his word and left every-thing to his nephew.

God, how Nancy loathed Jean! He had died almost forty years ago, but she wanted to kill him every day. He had stolen everything and ruined her life. Sunninghill, the Pavillon, the Palazzo Arichele, all lost. She even regretted the loss of some of the Jonson houses she would never have inherited, not unless lots of people had died, that is, which would have been a tragedy, except that at least she would have known how to live in them properly, which was more than could be said of some people she could name.

'All the lovely things, all the lovely houses,' said Nancy, 'where have they all gone?'

'Presumably the houses are where they've always been,' said Nicholas, 'but they're being lived in by people who can afford them.'

'But that's just it, I should be able to afford them!'

'Never use a conditional tense when it comes to money.'

Really, Nicholas was being impossible. She certainly wasn't going to tell him about her book. Ernest Hemingway had told Daddy that he really ought to write a book, because he told such funny stories. When Daddy protested that he couldn't write, Hemingway sent a tape-recorder. Daddy forgot to plug the thing in, and when the spools didn't go round, he lost his temper and threw it out of the window. Luckily, the woman it landed on didn't take any legal action and Daddy had another marvellous story, but the whole incident had made Nancy superstitious about tape-recorders. Maybe she should hire a ghost writer. Exorcized by a ghost! That would be original. Still, she had to give the poor ghost an idea of how she wanted it done. It could be theme by theme, or decade by decade, but that seemed to her a stuffy egghead bookworm kind of approach. She wanted it done sister by sister; after all, the rivalry between them was quite the dynamic force.

Gerty, the youngest and most beautiful of the three Jonson Sisters, was definitely the one Mummy was most competitive with. She married the Grand Duke Vladimir, nephew of the last Tsar of Russia. 'Uncle Vlad', as Nancy called him, had helped to assassinate Rasputin, lending his Imperial revolver to Prince Yussupov for what was supposed to be the final kill, but turned out to be only the middle stage between poisoning the energetic priest with arsenic and drowning him in the Neva. Despite many pleas, the Tsar exiled Vladimir for his part in the assassination, making him miss the Russian Revolution and the chance to get bayoneted, strangled or shot by Russia's new Bolshevik masters. Once in exile, Uncle Vlad went on to assassinate himself by drinking twenty-three dry martinis before lunch every day. Thanks to the Russian whimsy of smashing a glass after drinking from it, there was hardly a moment's silence in the house. Nancy had Daddy's copy of a forgotten memoir by Uncle Vlad's sister, the Grand Duchess Anna. It was inscribed in purple ink to 'my dear brother-in-law', although he was in fact her brother's sister-in-law's husband. The inscription seemed to Nancy somehow typical of the generous inclusiveness that had enabled that amazing family to straddle two continents, from Kiev to Vladivostok. Before Uncle Vlad's marriage to Gerty in Biarritz, his sister had to perform the blessing that would traditionally have been performed by their parents. It was a moment they dreaded because it reminded them of the horrifying reason for the absence of their family. The grand duchess described her feelings in *The Palace of Memory*:

> Through the window I could see the great
> waves pounding the rocks; the sun had gone
> down. The grey ocean at that moment looked
> to me as ruthless and indifferent as fate, and
> infinitely lonely.

Gerty decided to convert to the Russian Orthodox religion, in order to be closer to Vladimir's people. Anna went on:

> Our cousin, the Duke of Leuchtenberg, and I
> were her sponsors. The ceremony was a long
> and wearisome one, and I felt sorry for Gerty,
> who did not understand a word of it.

If her pet ghost could write as well as that, Nancy felt sure she would have a bestseller on her hands. The eldest Jonson Sister was the richest of all: bossy, practical Aunt Edith. While her flighty younger sisters jumped into the pages of an illustrated history book, holding hands with the remnants of some of the world's greatest families, sensible Aunt Edith, who preferred her antiques to arrive in a crate, made a consolidating marriage to a man whose father, like her own, had been on the list of the hundred richest men in America in 1900. Nancy spent the first two years of the war living with Edith, while Mummy tried to get some of her really valuable things into storage in Switzerland before joining her daughters in America. Edith's husband, Uncle Bill, struck an original note by paying with his own money for the presents he gave his wife. One birthday present was a white clapboard house with dark green shutters and two gently curved wings, on a slope of lawn above a lake, at the centre of a ten-thousand-acre plantation. She loved it. That was the sort of useful tip that they never gave you in books called *The Art of Giving*.

Patrick glanced at his unhappy aunt, still complaining to Nicholas by the entrance. He couldn't help thinking of the favourite dictum of the moderator from his Depression Group, 'Resentment is drinking the poison, and hoping that someone else will die'. All the patients had impersonated this sentence in more or less convincing Scottish accents at least once a day.

If he was now standing beside his mother's coffin with uneasy detachment, it was not because he had cherished his aunt's 'golden address book'. As far as Patrick was concerned, the past was a corpse waiting to be cremated, and although his wish was about to be granted in the most literal fashion, in a furnace only a few yards from where he was standing, another kind of fire was needed to incinerate the attitudes which haunted Nancy; the psychological impact of inherited wealth, the raging desire to get rid of it and the raging desire to hang on to it; the demoralizing effect of already having what almost everyone else was sacrificing their precious lives to acquire; the more or less secret superiority and the more or less secret shame of being rich, generating their characteristic disguises: the philanthropy solution, the alcoholic solution, the mask of eccentricity, the search for salvation in perfect taste; the defeated, the idle, and the frivolous, and their opponents, the standard-bearers, all living in a world that the dense glitter of alternatives made it hard for love and work to penetrate. If these values were in themselves sterile, they looked all the more ridiculous after two generations of disinheritance. Patrick wanted to distance himself from what he thought of as his aunt's virulent irrelevance, and yet there was a fascination with status running down the maternal line of his family that he had to understand.

He remembered going to see Eleanor just after she had launched her last philanthropic project, the Transpersonal Foundation. She had decided to renounce the frustration of being a person in favour of the exciting prospect of becoming a Transperson; denying part of what she was, the daughter of one bewildered family and the mother of another, and claiming to be what she was not, a healer and a saint. The impact of this adolescent project on her ageing body was to produce the first of the dozen strokes which eventually demolished her. When Patrick went down to see her in Lacoste after that first stroke, she was still able to speak fluently enough, but her mind had become entirely suspicious. The moment they were alone together in her bedroom, with the tattered curtains under full sail in the evening breeze, she clasped his arm and hissed to him urgently. 'Don't tell anybody my mother was a duchess.'

He nodded conspiratorially. She relaxed her grasp and searched the ceiling for the next worry.

Nancy's instructions, without even a stroke to justify them, would have been the exact opposite. Tell nobody? Tell everybody! Behind the cartoon contrasts of Nancy's worldliness and Eleanor's otherworldliness, Nancy's bulk and Eleanor's emaciation, there was a common cause, a past that had to be falsified, whether by suppression or selective glorification. What was that? Were Eleanor and Nancy individuals at all, or were they just part of the characteristic debris of their class and family?

Eleanor had taken Patrick to stay with her Aunt Edith in the early 1970s when he was twelve. While the rest of the world was worrying about the OPEC crisis, stagflation, carpet bombing and whether the effects of LSD were permanent, eternal or temporary, they found Edith living in a style which made no concession whatsoever to the fifty years since Live Oak had been given to her. The forty black servants made the slaves in *Gone With the Wind* look like extras on a film set. On the evening that Patrick and Eleanor arrived, Moses, one of the footmen, asked if he could be excused in order to go to his brother's funeral. Edith said no. There were four people at dinner and Moses was needed to serve the hominy grits. Patrick didn't mind if the servant who brought the quail, or the one who took the vegetables around, served the hominy grits as well, but there was a system in place and Edith was not going to allow it to be disrupted. Moses, in white gloves and a white coat, stepped forward silently, tears pouring down his cheeks, and offered Patrick his first taste of grits. He never knew if he would have liked them.

Later, beside a crackling fire in her bedroom, Eleanor raged against her aunt's cruelty. The scene over dinner had been too resonant for her; she could never disentangle the taste of the grits from Moses's tears, or indeed her mother's perfect taste from her own childhood tears. Eleanor's sense that her sanity was rooted in the kindness of servants meant that she would always be on Moses's side. If she had been articulate, this loyalty might have made her political; as it was it made her charitable. Most of all she raged against the way her aunt made her feel as if she were still twelve years old, as she had been when she was a passionate but mute guest at the beginning of the war, staying at Fairley, Bill and Edith's place on Long Island. His mother was hypnotized by the memory of being Patrick's age. Her arrested development always rigorously shadowed his efforts to grow up. In his early childhood she had been preoccupied by how much her nanny meant to her, while failing to provide him with a similar paragon of warmth and trustworthiness.

Looking up from his mother's coffin, Patrick saw that Nancy and Nicholas were planning to approach him again, their instinct for social hierarchy turning a bereaved son into the temporary top dog at his mother's funeral. He rested a hand on Eleanor's coffin, forming a secret alliance against misunderstanding.

'My dear,' said Nicholas, apparently refreshed by some important news, 'I hadn't realized, until Nancy enlightened me, what a serious partygoer your Mama used to be, before she took up her "good works".' He seemed to poke the phrase aside with his walking stick, clearing it from his path. 'To think of shy, religious little Eleanor at the Beistegui Ball! I didn't know her then, or I would have felt compelled to shield her from that stampede of ravenous harlequins.' Nicholas moved his free hand artistically through the air. 'It was a magical occasion, as if the gilded lay-abouts in one of Watteau's paintings had been released from their enchanted prison and given an enormous dose of steroids and a fleet of speedboats.'

'Oh, she wasn't all that shy, if you know what I'm saying,' Nancy corrected him. 'She had any number of beaux. You know your mother could have made a dazzling marriage.'

'And saved me the trouble of being born.'

'Oh, don't be so silly. You would have been born anyway.'

'Not quite.'

'When I think,' said Nicholas, 'of all the impostors who claim to have been at that legendary party, it's hard to believe that I knew someone who was there and chose never to mention it. And now it's too late to congratulate her on her modesty.' He patted the coffin, as an owner might pat a winning racehorse. 'Which shows the pointlessness of that particular affectation.'

Nancy spotted a white-haired man in a black pin-striped suit and a black silk tie walking down the aisle.

'Henry!' she said, staggering back theatrically. 'We needed some Jonson reinforcements.' Nancy loved Henry. He was so rich. It would have been better if the money had been hers, but a close relation having it was the next best thing.

'How are you, Cabbage?' she greeted him.

Henry kissed Nancy hello, without looking especially pleased to be addressed as 'Cabbage'.

'My God, I didn't expect to see you,' said Patrick. He felt a wave of remorse.

'I didn't expect to see you either,' said Henry. 'Nobody communicates in this family. I'm over here for a few days staying at the Connaught, and when they wheeled in *The Times* with my breakfast this morning, I saw that your mother had died and that there was a ceremony here today. Fortunately, the hotel got me a car straight away and I was able to make it.'

'I haven't seen you since you kindly had us to stay on your island,' said Patrick, deciding to plunge in. 'I think I was rather a nightmare. I'm sorry about that.'

'I guess nobody enjoys being unhappy,' said Henry.

'It always spills over. But we mustn't let a few foreign-policy differences get in the way of the really important things.'

'Absolutely,' said Patrick, struck by how kind Henry was being. 'I'm so glad you've made it here today. Eleanor was very fond of you.'

'Well, I loved your mother. As you know, she stayed with us at Fairley for a couple of years at the beginning of the war and so naturally we became very close. She had an innocent quality that was really attractive; it drew you in and at the same time it kept you at a certain distance. It's hard to explain, but whatever you feel about your mother and this charity she got involved with, I hope you know that she was a good person with the best intentions.'

'Yes,' said Patrick, accepting the simplicity of Henry's affection for a moment, 'I think "innocent" is exactly the right word.' He marvelled again at the effect of projection: how hostile Henry had seemed to him when Patrick was hostile towards everyone; how considerate he seemed now that Patrick had no argument with him. What would it be like to stop projecting? Was it possible at all?

As he turned to leave, Henry reached out and touched Patrick's shoulder.

'I'm sorry for your loss,' he said, with a formality that was by then infused with emotion. He nodded to Nancy and Nicholas.

'Excuse me,' said Patrick, looking back at the entrance of the crematorium, 'I have to say hello to Johnny Hall.'

'Who's he?' asked Nancy, sensing obscurity.

'You may well ask,' scowled Nicholas. 'He wouldn't be anybody at all, if he wasn't my daughter's psycho-analyst. As it is, he's a fiend.'

3

Patrick walked away from his mother's coffin, aware that unless he rushed back hysterically, he had stood beside her for the last time. He had seen the cold, damp contents of the coffin the night before, when he paid a visit to Bunyon's funeral parlour. A friendly, blue-suited woman with short white hair had greeted him at the door.

'Hello, love, I heard a taxi and I thought it was you.'

She guided him downstairs. Pink and brown diamond carpet like the bar of a country house hotel. Discreet advertisements for special services. A framed photograph of a woman kneeling by a black box from which a dove was only too pleased to be set free. Bolting upwards in a blur of white wings. Did it return to the Bunyon's dovecote and get recycled? Oh, no, not the black box again. 'We can release a dove for you on the day of your funeral'. Gothic script seemed to warp every letter that passed through the door of the funeral parlour, as if death were a German village. There were stained-glass windows, electrically lit, on the stairs down to the basement.

'I'll leave you with her. If there's anything you need, don't hesitate. I'll be upstairs.'

'Thank you,' said Patrick, waiting for her to turn the corner before stepping into the Willow Chapel.

He closed the door behind him and glanced hurriedly into the coffin, as though his mother had told him it was rude to stare. Whatever he was looking at, it was not the 'her' he had been promised with solemn cosiness a few minutes before. The absence of life in that familiar body, the rigid and rectified features of the face he had known before he even knew his own, made all the difference. Here was a transitional object for the far end of life. Instead of the soft toy or raggie that a child uses to cope with its mother's absence, he was being offered a corpse, its scrawny fingers clutching an artificial white rose whose stiff silk petals were twisted into position over an unbeating heart. It had the sarcasm of a relic, as well as the prestige of a metonym. It stood for his mother and for her absence with equal authority. In either case, it was her final appearance before she retired into other people's memory.

He had better take another look, a longer look, a less theoretical look, but how could he concentrate in this disconcerting basement? The Willow Chapel turned out to be under a busy pavement, pierced by the declamatory brightness of mobile-phone talk and tattooed by clicking heels. A rumbling taxi emerged from the general traffic and splashed a puddle onto the paving stones above the far corner of the ceiling. He was reminded of the Tennyson poem he hadn't thought of for decades, 'Dead, long dead, / Long dead! / And my heart is a handful of dust, / And the wheels go over my head, / And my bones are shaken with pain, / For in a shallow grave they are thrust, / Only a yard beneath the street, / And the hoofs of the horses beat, beat, / The hoofs of the horses beat, / Beat into my scalp and my brain, / With never an end to the stream of passing feet.' He could see why Bunyon's had chosen to call this room the Willow Chapel rather than the Coal Cellar or the Shallow Grave. 'Hello, love, your Mum's in the Coal Cellar,' muttered Patrick. 'We could release a dove in the Shallow Grave, but it would have no chance whatever of escape.' He sat down and rocked his torso over his folded arms. His entrails were in torment, as they had been since hearing about his mother's death three days ago. No need for ten years of psychoanalysis to work out that he felt 'gutted'. He was doing what he always did under pressure, observing everything, chattering to himself in different voices, circling the unacceptable feelings, in this case conveniently embedded in his mother's coffin.

She had left the world with screeching slowness, sliding inch by inch into oblivion. At first he could not help enjoying the comparative quiet of her presence, but then he noticed that he was clinging to the urban noises outside in order not to be drawn into the deep pit of silence at the centre of the room. He must take a closer look, but first he really had to turn down the lights that were glaring through chrome grids in the low polystyrene ceiling. They bleached the glow of the four stout candles impaled on brass stands at the corners of the coffin. He dimmed the spotlights and restored some of the ecclesiastical pomposity to the candles. There was one more thing he had to check. A pink velvet curtain partitioned the room; he had to know what was behind it before he could pay attention to his mother. It turned out to hide a storage area packed with equipment: a grey metal trolley with sensible wheels, some no-nonsense rubber tubes and a huge gold crucifix. Everything needed to embalm a Christian. Eleanor had expected to meet Jesus at the end of a tunnel after she died. The poor man was a slave to his fans, waiting to show crowds of eager dead the neon countryside that lay beyond the rebirth canal of earthly annihilation. It must be hard to be chosen as optimism's master cliché, the Light at the End of the Tunnel, ruling over a glittering army of half-full glasses and silver-lined clouds.

Patrick let the curtain drop reluctantly, acknowledging that he had run out of distractions. He edged towards the coffin, like a man approaching a cliff. At least he knew that this coffin contained his mother's corpse. Twenty years ago, when he had been to see his father's remains in New York, he was shown into the wrong room. 'In loving memory of Hermann Newton'. He had done everything he could to opt out of that bereavement process, but he was not going to evade this one. A cool dry part of his mind was trying to bring his emotions under its aphoristic sway, but the stabbing pain in his guts undermined its ambitions, and confused his defences.

As he stared into the coffin, he felt the encroachment of an agitated animal sadness. He wanted to linger incredulously by the body, still giving it some of the attention it had commanded in life: a shake, a touch, a word, an enquiring gaze. He reached out and put his hand on her chest and felt the shock of its thinness. He leant over and kissed her on the forehead and felt the shock of its coldness. These sharp sensations lowered his defences further, and he was overwhelmed by an expanding rush of sympathy for the ruined human being in front of him. During its fleeting life, this vast sense of tenderness reduced his mother's personality to a detail, and his relationship with her to a detail within a detail.

He sat down again and leant forward over his crossed legs and folded arms to give himself some faint relief from the pain in his stomach. And then he suddenly made a connection. Of course, how strange – how determined. Aged seven, going on his first trip alone abroad with his mother, a few months after his parents' divorce. His first flash of Italy: the white number plates, the blue bay, the ochre churches. They were staying at the Excelsior in Naples, on a waterfront buzzing with waspish motorcycles and humming with crowded trams. From the balcony of their magnificent room, his mother pointed to the street urchins crouched on the roofs, or clinging to the backs of the trams. Patrick, who thought they were in Naples on holiday, was alarmed to hear that Eleanor had come there to save these poor children. There was a marvellous man, a priest called Father Tortelli, who never tired of picking up lost Neapolitan boys and giving them shelter in the refuge that Eleanor had been bankrolling from London. She was now going to see it for the first time. Wasn't it exciting? Wasn't it a good thing to be doing? She showed Patrick a photograph of Father Tortelli: a small, tough, fifty-year-old man in a black shirt who looked as if he was no stranger to the boxing ring. His bearish arms were locked around the fragile, sharp-boned shoulders of two sun-tanned boys in white vests. Father Tortelli was protecting them from the streets, but who was protecting them from Father Tortelli? Not Eleanor. She was providing him with the means to fill his refuge with ever-growing numbers of orphans and runaways. After lunch that day, Patrick had an attack of violent gastro-enteritis, and instead of leaving him in luxurious neglect while she went to look after the other children, his mother was made to stay with him and hold his hand while he screamed with pain in the green marble bathroom.

No amount of stomach ache could make her stay

now. Not that he wanted her to stay, but his body had a memory of its own which it continued to narrate without any reference to his current wishes. What was it that had driven Eleanor to furnish children for her husband and for Father Tortelli, and why was the drive so strong that, after the collapse of her marriage, she immediately replaced a father with a Father, a doctor with a priest? Patrick had no doubt that her motives were unconscious, as unconscious as the somatic memory that had taken him over in the last three days. What could he do but drag these fragments out of the dark and acknowledge them?

After a quiet knock, the door opened and the attendant leant into the room.

'Just to make sure everything is all right,' she whispered.

'Maybe it is,' said Patrick.

The journey back to his flat had a mildly hallucinatory quality, surging through the rainy night in a fluorescent bus, freshly flooded by so many fierce impressions and remote memories. There were two Jehovah's Witnesses on board, a black man handing out leaflets and a black woman preaching at the top of her voice. 'Repent of your sins and take Jesus into your heart, because when you die it will be too late to repent in the grave and you'll burn in the fires of Hell . . .'

A red-eyed Irishman in a threadbare tweed jacket started shouting in counterpoint from a back seat. 'Shut up, you fuckin' bitch. Go suck Satan's cock. You're not allowed to do this, whether you're Muslim, or Christian, or Satanic.' When the man with the leaflets headed for the upper deck, he persisted, investing his accent with a sadistic Southern twang, 'I can see you, Boy. How do you think you'd look with your head under your arm, Boy. If you don't shut that bitch up, I'll adjust your face for you, Boy.'

'Oh, do shut up yourself,' said an exasperated commuter.

Patrick noticed that his stomach pains had gone. He watched the Irishman sway in his seat, his lips continuing to argue silently with the Jehovah's Witness, or with some Jesuit from his youth. Give us a boy till the age of seven and we'll have him for life. Not me, thought Patrick, you won't have me.

As the bus pushed haltingly towards his destination, he thought about those brief but pivotal nights in the Suicide Observation Room, unpeeling one sweat-soaked T-shirt after another, throwing off the sauna of the bedclothes only to shudder in the freezer of their absence; turning the light on and off, pained by the brightness, alarmed by the dark; a poisonous headache lurching around his skull like the lead in a jumping bean. He had brought nothing to read except *The Tibetan Book of the Dead*, hoping to find its exotic iconography ridiculous enough to purge any fantasies he might still cling to about consciousness continuing after death. As it turned out, he found his imagination seduced by a passage from the introduction to the *Chonyid Bardo*, 'O nobly born, when thy body and thy mind were separating, thou must have experienced a glimpse of the Pure Truth, subtle, sparkling, bright, dazzling, glorious and radiantly awesome, in appearance like a mirage moving across a landscape in springtime in one continuous stream of vibrations. Be not daunted thereby, nor terrified, nor awed. That is the radiance of thine own true nature. Recognize it.'

The words had a psychedelic authority that over-powered the materialist annihilation he longed to believe in. He struggled to restore his faith in the finality of death, but couldn't help seeing it as a superstition among superstitions, no more bracingly rational than the rest. The idea that an afterlife had been invented to reassure people who couldn't face the finality of death was no more plausible than the idea that the finality of death had been invented to reassure people who couldn't face the nightmare of endless experience. His delirium tremens collaborated with the poets of the *Bardo* to produce a sensation of seething electrocution as he was goaded towards the abattoir of sleep, terrified that the slaughter of his rational mind would present him with a 'glimpse of the Pure Truth'.

Memories and phrases loomed and flitted like fog banks on a night road. Thoughts threatened him from a distance, but disappeared as he approached them. 'Drowned in dreams and burning to be gone'. Who had said that? Other people's words. Had he already thought 'other people's words'? Things seemed far away and then, a moment later, repetitious. Was it like fog, or was it more like hot sand, something he was labouring through and trying not to touch at the same time? Cold and wet, hot and dry. How could it be both? How could it be other than both? Similes of dissimilarities – another phrase that seemed to chase itself like a miniature train around a tight circuit. Please make it stop.

A scene that kept tumbling back into his delirious thoughts was his visit to the philosopher Victor Eisen after Victor's near-death experience. He had found his old Saint-Nazaire neighbour in the London clinic, still strapped to the machines that had flat-lined a few days earlier. Victor's withered yellow arms emerged limply from an institutional dressing gown, but as he described what had happened his speech was as rapid and emphatic as ever, saturated by a lifetime of confident opinions.

'I came to a riverbank and on the other side was a red light which controlled the universe. There were two figures either side of it, who I knew to be the Lord of Time and the Lord of Space. They communicated to me directly through their thoughts, without using any speech. They told me that the fabric of Time-Space was torn and that I had to repair it, that the fate of the universe depended on me. I had a tremendous sense of urgency and purpose and I was on my way to fulfil my task when I felt myself being dragged back into my body and I very reluctantly returned.'

For three weeks Victor was won over by the feeling of authenticity that accompanied his vision, but then the habits of his public atheism and the fear that the logical reductions enshrined in his philosophical work might be invalidated made him squeeze his new sense of openness back into the biological crisis he was suffering at the time. He decided that the pressing mission he had been sent on by the controller of the universe was an allegory of a brain running out of oxygen. His mind had been failing, not expanding.

As he lay sweating in that narrow room, thinking about Victor's need to decide what everything meant, Patrick wondered if he could ever make his ego light enough to relax in not having to settle the meaning of things. What would that feel like?

In the meantime, the Suicide Observation Room lived up to its majestic name. In it, he saw that suicide had always formed the unquestioned backdrop to his existence. Even before he had taken to carrying around a copy of *The Myth of Sisyphus* in his overcoat pocket, making its first sentence the mantra of his early twenties, Patrick had greeted the day with the basic question, 'Can anyone think of a good reason not to kill himself?' Since he lived at the time in a theatrical solitude, crowded with mad and mocking voices, he was not likely to get an affirmative answer. Elaborate postponement was the best he could hope for, and in the end the obligation to talk proved stronger than the desire to die. During the next twenty years the suicidal chatter died down to an occasional whisper on a coastal path, or in a quiet chemist. When it returned in full force, it took the form of a grim monologue rather than a surreal chorus. The comparative simplicity of the most recent assault made him realize that he had only ever been superficially in love with easeful death and was much more deeply enthralled by his own personality. Suicide wore the mask of self-rejection; but in reality nobody took their personality more seriously than the person who was planning to kill himself on its instructions. Nobody was more determined to stay in charge at any cost, to force the most mysterious aspect of life into their own imperious schedule.

His month in the Priory had been a crucial period of his life, transforming the crisis that had led to the breakdown of his marriage and the escalation of his drinking. It was disquieting to think how close he had come to running away after only three days, lured by Becky's departure. Before leaving, she had found him in the lounge of the Depression Wing.

'I was looking for you. I'm not meant to speak to anyone,' she said in a mock whisper, 'because I'm a bad influence.'

She gave him a little folded note and a light kiss on the lips before hurrying out of the room.

This is my sister's address. She's away in the States, so I'll be there alone, if you feel like running away from this fucking place and doing something CRAZY. Love Becks.

The note reminded him of the jagged CRAZYs he used to doodle in the margins of his O-level chemistry notes after smoking a joint during the morning break at school. It was out of the question to visit her, he told himself, as he called a minicab service listed in the payphone booth under the back stairs. Was this what they meant by powerless?

'Just don't!' he muttered, closing the door of his minicab firmly to show how determined he was not to pursue a bloodstained festival of dysfunction. He gave the driver the address on Becky's note.

'Well, you must be all right if they let you out,' said the jaunty driver.

'I let myself out. I couldn't afford it.'

'Bit pricey, is it?'

Patrick didn't answer, glazed over with desire and conflict.

'Have you heard the one about the man who goes into the psychiatrist's office?' asked the driver, setting off down the drive and smiling in the rear-view mirror. 'He says, "It's been terrible, Doctor, for three years

I thought I was a butterfly, and that's not all, it gets worse: for the last three months I thought I was a moth." "Good God," says the psychiatrist, "what a difficult time you've been having. So, what made you come here today and ask for help?" "Well," says the man, "I saw the light in the window and I felt drawn to it, so I just flew in."'

'That's a good one,' said Patrick, sinking deeper into Becky's imagined nakedness, while wondering how long his latest dose of oxazepam would last. 'Do you specialize in Priory patients because of your sunny temperament?'

'You say that,' said the driver, 'but last year for about four months I literally couldn't get out of bed, literally couldn't see the point in anything.'

'Oh, I'm sorry,' said Patrick.

From Hammersmith Broadway to the Shepherd's Bush roundabout, they talked about the causeless weeping, the suicidal daydreams, the excruciating slowness, the sleepless nights and the listless days. By the time they reached Bayswater, they were best friends and the driver turned round to Patrick and said with the full blast of his restored cheerfulness, 'In a few months you'll be looking back on what you've just been through and saying, "*What* was all that about? What was all that fuss and aggravation about?" That's what happened to me.'

Patrick looked back down at Becky's note. She had signed herself with the name of a beer. Becks. He started to whisper hoarsely under his breath, in a Marlon Brando as Vito Corleone voice, 'The one who comes to you and asks for a meeting, and has the same name as a well-known brand of beer – *she's* the one that wants you to have a relapse . . .'

Not the voices, he mustn't let them kick off. 'It starts off with a little Marlon Brando impersonation,' sighed Mrs. Mop, 'and the next thing you know . . .'

'Shut up!' Patrick interrupted.

'What?'

'Oh, not you. I'm sorry.'

They turned into a big square with a central garden. The driver drew up to a white stucco building. Patrick leant sideways and looked out of the window. Becky was on the third floor, beautiful, available and mentally ill.

To think of the things he'd done for a little intimacy, earth flying over his shoulder as he dug his own grave. There were the good women who gave him the care he had never had. They had to be tortured into letting him down, to show that they couldn't really be trusted. And then there were the bad women who saved time by being untrustworthy straight away. He generally alternated between these two broad categories, enchanted by some variant which briefly masked the futility of defending the decaying fortress of his personality, while hoping that it would obligingly rearrange itself into a temple of peace and fulfilment. Hoping and moping, moping and hoping. With only a little detachment, his love life looked like a child's wind-up toy made to march again and again over the precipice of a kitchen table. Romance was where love was most under threat, not where it was likely to achieve its highest expression. If a candidate was sufficiently hopeless, like Becky, she took on the magnetism of the obviously doomed. It was embarrassing to be so deluded, and even more embarrassing to react to the delusion, like a man running away from his own looming shadow.

'I know this sounds a little bit *crazy*, for want of a better word,' said Patrick with a snort of laughter, 'but do you think you could drive me back? I'm not ready yet.'

'Back to the Priory?' said the driver, no longer quite as sympathetic to his passenger.

He doesn't want to know about those of us who

have to go back, thought Patrick. He closed his eyes
and stretched out in the back seat. 'Talk would talk
and go so far askance . . . something, something . . .
You don't want madhouse and the whole thing there.'
The whole thing there. The wonderful inarticulacy of
it, expanding with threat and contracting with osten-
sive urgency.

On the drive back, Patrick started to feel chest
pains which even the violence of his longing for pathological romance could no longer explain. His hands
were shaking and he could feel the sweat breaking out
on his forehead. By the time he reached Dr. Pagazzi's
office, he was hallucinating mildly and apparently
trapped in a two-dimensional space with no depth,
like an insect crawling around a window pane, looking
for a way out. Dr. Pagazzi scolded him for missing his
four o'clock dose of oxazepam, saying that he might
have a heart attack if he withdrew too fast. Patrick
lifted the dull plastic tub in his shaking hand and
knocked back three oxazepam.

The next day he 'shared' his near escape with the
Depression Group. It turned out that all of them had
nearly run away, or had run away and come back, or
thought about running away much of the time. Some,
on the other hand, dreaded leaving, but they only

seemed superficially opposite to the ones who wanted to run away: everyone was obsessed with how much therapy they needed before they could begin a 'normal life'. Patrick was surprised by how grateful he felt for the sense of solidarity with the other patients. A lifelong habit of being set apart was briefly overturned by a wave of goodwill towards everyone in the group.

Johnny Hall had taken an unassuming seat near the back of the room. Patrick worked his way round the far end of the pew to join his old friend.

'How are you bearing up?' said Johnny.

'Pretty well,' said Patrick, sitting down next to him. 'I have a strange feeling of excitement which I wouldn't admit to anyone except you and Mary. I felt rather knocked out for the first few days, but then I had what I think your profession would call an "insight". I went to the funeral parlour yesterday evening and sat with Eleanor's body. I connected . . . I'll tell you later.'

Johnny smiled encouragingly. 'Christ,' he said, after a pause, 'Nicholas Pratt. I didn't expect to see him.'

'Neither did I. You're so lucky to have an ethical reason not to talk to him.'

'Doesn't everybody?'

'Quite.'

'I'll see you afterwards at the Onslow,' said Johnny, leaving Patrick to the usher who had come up to him and was standing by expectantly.

'We can start whenever you're ready, sir,' said the usher, somehow hinting at the queue of corpses that would pile up unless the ceremony got going right away.

Patrick scanned the room. There were a few dozen people sitting in the pews facing Eleanor's coffin.

'Fine,' he said, 'let's begin in ten minutes.'

'Ten minutes?' said the usher, like a young child who has been told he can do something really exciting when he's twenty-one.

'Yes, there are still people arriving,' said Patrick, noticing Julia standing in the doorway, a spiky effusion of black against the dull morning: black veil, black hat, stiff black silk dress and, he imagined, softer black silk beneath. He immediately felt the impact of her mentality, that intense but exclusive sensitivity. She was like a spider's web, trembling at the slightest touch, but indifferent to the light that made its threads shine in the wet grass.

'You're just in time,' said Patrick, kissing Julia through her scratchy black veil.

'You mean late as usual.'

'No; just in time. We're about to kick off, if that's the phrase I'm looking for.'

'It's not,' she said, with that short husky laugh that always got to him.

The last time they had seen each other was in the French hotel where their affair had ended. Despite their communicating rooms, they could think of nothing to say to each other. Sitting through long meals, under the vault of an artificial sky, painted with faint clouds and garlands of tumbling roses, they stared at a flight of steps that led down to the slapping keels of a private harbour, ropes creaking against bollards, bollards rusting into stone quays; everything longing to leave.

'Now that you're not with Mary, you don't need me. I was . . . structural.'

'Exactly.'

The single word was perhaps too bare and could only be outstripped by silence. She had stood up and walked away without further comment. A gull launched itself from the soiled balustrade and clapped its way out to sea with a piercing cry. He had wanted to call her back, but the impulse died in the thick carpet lengthening between them.

Looking at him now, the freshly bereaved son, Julia decided she felt utterly detached from Patrick, apart from wanting him to find her irresistible.

'I haven't seen you for such a long time,' said Patrick, looking down at Julia's lips, red under the black net of her veil. He remained inconveniently attracted to almost all the women he had ever been to bed with, even when he had a strong aversion to a revival on all other grounds.

'A year and a half,' said Julia. 'Is it true that you've given up drinking? It must be hard just now.'

'Not at all: a crisis demands a hero. The ambush comes when things are going well, or so I'm told.'

'If you can't speak personally about things going well, they haven't changed that much.'

'They have changed, but my speech patterns may take a while to catch up.'

'I can't wait.'

'If there's an opportunity for irony . . .'

'You'll take it.'

'It's the hardest addiction of all,' said Patrick. 'Forget heroin. Just try giving up irony, that deep-down need to mean two things at once, to be in two places at once, not to be there for the catastrophe of a fixed meaning.'

'Don't!' said Julia, 'I'm having enough trouble wearing nicotine patches and still smoking at the same time. Don't take away my irony,' she pleaded, clasping him histrionically, 'leave me with a little sarcasm.'

'Sarcasm doesn't count. It only means one thing: contempt.'

'You always were a quality freak,' said Julia. 'Some of us like sarcasm.'

Julia noticed that she was playing with Patrick. She felt a small tug of nostalgia, but reminded herself sternly that she was well rid of him. Besides, she had Gunther now, a charming German banker who spent the middle of the week in London. It was true that he was married, as Patrick had been, but in every other way he was the opposite: slick, fit, rich and disciplined. He had opera tickets, and bookings in caviar bars and membership of nightclubs, organized by his personal assistant. Sometimes he threw caution to the winds and put on his ironed jeans and his zip-up suede jacket and took her to jazz clubs in unusual parts of town, always, of course, with a big, reassuring, silent car waiting outside to take them back to Hays Mews, just behind Berkeley Square, where Gunther, like all his friends, was having a swimming pool put into the sub-basement of his triple mews house lateral conversion.

He collected hideous contemporary art with the haphazard credulity of a man who has friends in the art world. There were artistic black-and-white photographs of women's nipples in his dressing room. He made Julia feel sophisticated, but he didn't make her want to play. The thought simply didn't enter her head when she was with Gunther. He had never struggled to give up irony. He knew, of course, that it existed and he pursued it doggedly with all the silliness at his command.

'We'd better find a seat,' said Patrick. 'I'm not quite sure what's going on; I haven't even had time to look at the order of service.'

'But didn't you organize it?'

'No. Mary did.'

'Sweet!' said Julia. 'She's always so helpful, more like a mother than your own mother really.'

Julia felt her heart rate accelerate; perhaps she had gone too far. She was amazed that her old competition with that paragon of self-sacrifice had suddenly burst out, now that it was so out of date.

'She was, until she had children of her own,' said Patrick amiably. 'That rather blew my cover.'

From fearing that he would take offence, Julia found herself wishing he would stop being so maddeningly calm.

Organ music purred into life.

'Well, real or not, I have to burn the remains of the only mother I'll ever have,' said Patrick, smiling briskly at Julia and setting off down the aisle to the front row where Mary was keeping a seat for him.

4

Mary sat in the front pew of the crematorium staring at Eleanor's coffin, mastering a moment of rebellion. Wondering where Patrick was, she had looked back and seen him bantering flirtatiously with Julia. Now that nothing serious depended on her cultivated indifference, she felt a thud of exasperation. Here she was again, being helpful, while Patrick, in one of the more legitimate throes of his perpetual crisis, bestowed his attention on another woman. Not that she wanted more of his attention; all she wanted from Patrick was for him to be a little freer, a little less predictable. To be fair, and she sometimes wished she could stop being so fair, that's what he wanted as well. She had to remind herself that separation had made them grow closer. No longer hurled together or driven apart by their habitual reactions, they had settled into a relatively stable orbit around the children and around each other.

Her irritation was further blunted when a second backward glance yielded a grave smile from Erasmus Price, her own tiny concession to the consolations of adultery. She had started her affair with him in the South of France, where Patrick had insisted on renting a house during the final disintegration of their marriage, compulsively circling back to the area around his childhood home in Saint-Nazaire. Mary protested against this extravagance in vain; Patrick was in the last phase of his drinking, stumbling around the labyrinth of his unconscious, unavailable for discussion.

The Prices, whose own marriage was falling apart, had sons roughly the same age as Robert and Thomas. Despite these promising symmetries, harmony eluded the two families.

'Anybody who is amazed that "a week is a long time in politics",' said Patrick on the second day, 'should try having the Prices to stay. It turns out to be a fucking eternity. Do you know how he got his wacky name? His father was in the middle of editing the sixty-five-volume Oxford University Press *Complete Works of Erasmus* when his mother interrupted him with the news that she had given birth to a son. "Let's call him Erasmus," he cried, like a man inspired, "or Luther, whose crucial letter to Erasmus I was re-reading only this morning." Given the choice . . .' Patrick subsided.

Mary ignored him, knowing that he was just setting up that day's pretext for more senseless drinking. After Patrick had passed out and Emily Price had gone to bed, Mary sat up late, listening to Erasmus's troubles.

'Some people think that the future belongs to them and that they can lose it,' he said on the first evening, staring into his wine-dark glass, 'but I don't have that sense at all. Even when the work is going well, I wouldn't mind if I could painlessly and instantly expire.'

Why was she drawn to these gloomy men? As a philosopher, at least Erasmus, like Schopenhauer, could make his pessimism into a world view. He cheered up at the mention of the German philosopher.

'My favourite remark of his was the advice he gave to a dying friend: "You are ceasing to be something you would have done better never to become."'

'That must have helped,' said Mary.

'A real nostalgia-buster,' he whispered admiringly.

According to Erasmus his marriage was irreparable;

the puzzle for Mary was that it existed at all. As a guest, Emily Price had three main drawbacks: she was incapable of saying please, incapable of saying thank you and incapable of saying sorry, all the while creating a surge in the demand for these expressions. When she saw Mary applying sunblock to Thomas's sharp pale shoulders, she hurried over and scooped the white cream out of Mary's cupped hand, saying, 'I can't see it without wanting to take some.' By her own account, the same hunger had haunted the birth of her eldest son: 'The moment I saw him, I thought: *I want another one.*'

Emily complained about Cambridge, she complained about her husband and about her sons, she complained about her house, she complained about France and the sun and the clouds and the leaves and the wind and the bottle tops. She couldn't stop; she had to bail out the flooding dinghy of her discontent. Sometimes she set false targets with her complaining: Cambridge was hell, London was great, but when Erasmus applied for a job at London University, she made him withdraw. At the time, she had said that he was too cowardly to apply, but on holiday with the Melroses she admitted the truth. 'I only wanted to move to London so I could complain about the air quality and the schools.'

Patrick was momentarily jolted out of his stupor by the challenge of Emily's personality.

'She could be the centrepiece of a Kleinian Conference – "Talk About Bad Breasts".' He giggled sweatily on the bed while Mary cultivated patience. 'She had a difficult start in life,' he sighed. 'Her mother wouldn't let her use the biros in their house, in case they ran out of ink.' He fell off the bed laughing, knocked his head on the bedside table and had to take a handful of codeine to deal with the bump.

When Mary abandoned tolerance, she did it vehemently. She could feel Emily's underlying sense of privation like the blast from a furnace, but she somehow made the decision to put aside her characteristic empathy, to stay with the annoying consequences and not to feel the distressing causes of Emily's behaviour, especially after Erasmus's clumsy pass, which she hadn't entirely rejected, on the second evening of their endless conversation about marital failure. For a week, they kept each other afloat with the wreckage from their respective marriages. On their return to England it took them two months to admit the futility of trying to build an affair out of these sodden fragments — just long enough for Mary to struggle loyally through Erasmus's latest work, *None the Wiser: Developments in the Philosophy of Consciousness*.

It was the presence of *None the Wiser* on Mary's bedside table that alerted Patrick to his wife's laborious romance.

'You couldn't be reading that book unless you were having an affair with the author,' he guessed through half-closed eyes.

'Believe me, it's virtually impossible even then.'

He gave in to the relief of closing his eyes completely, a strange smile on his lips. She realized with vague disgust that he was pleased to have the huge weight of his infidelity alleviated by her trivial contribution to the other side of the scales.

After that, there was what her mother would have called an 'absolutely maddening' period, when Patrick only emerged from his new blackout bedsit in order to lecture or interrogate her about consciousness studies, sometimes with the slow sentential precision of drunkenness, sometimes with its visionary fever, all delivered with the specious fluency of a man used to pleading a case in public.

'The subject of consciousness, in order to enter the realm of science, must become the object of consciousness, and that is precisely what it cannot do, for the eye cannot perceive itself, cannot vault from its socket fast enough to glimpse the lens. The language of experience and the language of experiment hang like oil and water in the same test tube, never mingling except from the violence of philosophy. The violence of philosophy. Would you agree? Whoops. Don't worry about that lamp, I'll get you a new one.

'Seriously, though, where do you stand on microtubules? Microtubular bells. Are you For or Against? Do you think that a theory of extended mind can base itself confidently in quantum non-locality? Do you believe that two linked particles conceived in the warm spiralling quantum womb of a microtubule could continue to inform each other as they rush through vast fields of interstellar darkness; still communicating despite the appearance of *icy separation*? Are you For, or Against? And what difference would it make to experience if these particles did continue to resonate with each other, since it is not particles that we experience?'

'Oh, for God's sake shut up.'

'Who will rid us of the Explanatory Gap?' he shouted, like Henry II requesting an assassin for his troublesome priest. 'And is that gap just a product of our misconstrued discourse?' He ploughed on, 'Is reality a consensual hallucination? And is a nervous breakdown in fact a *refusal to consent*? Go on, don't be shy, tell me what you think.'

'Why don't you go back to your flat and pass out there? I don't want the children seeing you in this state.'

'What state? A state of philosophical enquiry? I thought you would approve.'

'I've got to collect the boys. Please go home.'

'How sweet that you think of it as my home. I'm not in that happy position.'

He would leave, abandoning the consciousness debate for a slamming door. Even 'fucking bitch' had a welcome directness after the twisted use he made of abstract phrases like 'property dualism' to express his shattered sense of home. She felt less and less guilty about his stormy departures. She dreaded Robert and Thomas asking her about their father's moods, his glaring silences, his declamatory introversion, the spectacle of his clumsiness and misery. The children in fact saw very little of him. He was 'away on business' for the last two months of his drinking and for his month in the Priory. With his unusual talent for mimicry,

Robert still managed to impersonate the concerns that Erasmus wrote books about and Patrick used to make veiled attacks on his wife.

'Where do thoughts come from?' he muttered, pacing up and down pensively. 'Before you decide to move your hand where does the decision live?'

'Honestly, Bobby,' said Thomas, letting out a short giggle. 'I expect Brains would know.'

'Well, Mr. Tracy,' stammered Robert, bobbing up and down on imaginary strings, 'when you move your hand, your . . . your brain tells you to move your hand, but what tells your brain to tell your hand?'

'That's a real puzzle, Brains,' said Robert, switching to Mr. Tracy's basso profundo.

'Weh-well, Mr. Tracy,' he returned to the stammering scientist, 'I've invented a machine that may be able to s-solve that puzzle. It's called the Thinkatron.'

'Switch it on, switch it on!' shouted Thomas, swishing his raggie in the air.

Robert made a loud humming sound that gradually grew more threatening.

'Oh, no, it's going to blow up!' warned Thomas. 'The Thinkatron is going to blow up!'

Robert flung himself on the floor with the sound of a huge explosion.

'Gee, Mr. Tracy, I guess I must have o-overloaded the primary circuits.'

'Don't worry, Brains,' said Thomas magnanimously, 'I'm sure you'll work it out. But seriously,' he added to Mary, 'what is the "consciousness debate" that Dada gets so angry about?'

'Oh, God,' said Mary, desperate for someone close to her who didn't want to talk about consciousness. She thought she could put Thomas off by making the subject sound impenetrably learned. 'It's really the philosophical and scientific debate about whether the brain and the mind are identical.'

'Well, of course not,' said Thomas taking his thumb out of his mouth and rounding his eyes, 'I mean, the brain is part of the body and the mind is the outer soul.'

'Quite,' said Mary, amazed.

'What I don't understand,' said Thomas, 'is why things exist.'

'What do you mean? Why there's something rather than nothing?'

'Yes.'

'I have no idea, but it's probably worth staying surprised by that.'

'I am surprised by it, Mama. I'm really surprised.'

When she told Erasmus what Thomas had said about the mind being the 'outer soul', he didn't seem as impressed as she had been.

'It's rather an old-fashioned view,' he commented, 'although the more modern point of view, that the soul is the inner mind, can't be said to have got us anywhere by simply inverting the relationship between two opaque signifiers.'

'Right,' said Mary. 'Still, don't you think it's rather extraordinary for a six-year-old to be so clear about that famously tricky subject?'

'Children often say things that seem extraordinary to us precisely because the big questions are not yet "famously tricky" for them. Oliver is obsessed with death at the moment and he's also only six. He can't bear it, it hasn't become part of How It Is; it's still a scandal, a catastrophic design flaw; it ruins everything. We've got used to the fact of death – although the experience is irreducibly strange. He hasn't found the trick of putting a hood on the executioner, of hiding the experience with the fact. He still sees it as pure experience. I found him crying over a dead fly lying on the windowsill. He asked me why things have to die and all I could offer him was tautology: because nothing lasts for ever.'

Erasmus's need to take a general and theoretical view of every situation sometimes infuriated Mary. All she had wanted was a little compliment for Thomas. Even when she finally told him that she felt there was no point in carrying on with their affair, he accepted her position with insulting equanimity, and then went on to admit that he had 'recently been toying with the Panpsychist approach', as if this unveiling of the wild side of his intellect might tempt her to change her mind.

Mary had decided not to take the children to Eleanor's funeral, but to leave them with her mother. Thomas had no memory of Eleanor and Robert was so steeped in his father's sense of betrayal that the occasion would be more likely to revive faded hostility than to relieve a natural sense of sadness and loss. They had all been together for the last time about two years before in Kew Gardens, during the bluebell season, soon after Eleanor had come back from Saint-Nazaire to live in England. On their way to the Woodland Walk, Mary pushed Eleanor's wheelchair through the twisting Rhododendron Dell, hemmed in by walls of outrageous colour. Patrick hung back, gulping down the odd miniature of Johnnie Walker Black Label in moments of feigned fascination with a sprawling pink or orange blossom, while Robert and Thomas explored the gigantic bushes ranged against the slopes on either side. When a golden pheasant emerged onto the path, its saffron-yellow and blood-red feathers shining like enamel, Mary stopped the wheelchair, astonished. The pheasant crossed the hot cinder with the bobbing majesty of an avian gait, the price of a strained talent, like the high head of a swimming dog. Eleanor, crumpled in her seat, wearing old baby-blue flannel trousers and a maroon cardigan with big flat buttons and holes at the elbow, stared at the bird with the alarmed distaste that had taken up residence in her frozen features. Patrick, determined not to talk to his mother, hurried past muttering that he'd 'better keep an eye on the boys'.

Eleanor gestured frantically to Mary to come closer and then produced one of her rare whole sentences.

'I can never forget that he's David's son.'

'I don't think it's his father who haunts him these days,' said Mary, surprised by her own sharpness.

'Haunts . . .' said Eleanor.

Mary was thrusting the wheelchair through the dappled potholes of the Woodland Walk by the time Eleanor was able to speak again.

'Are . . . you . . . all . . . right?'

She asked the same question again and again, with mounting agitation, ignoring the haze of bluebells, mingled with the yellow stalks of wild garlic, under the shifting and swelling shade of the oaks. She was trying to save Mary from Patrick, not out of any insight into her circumstances, but in order to save herself, by some retroactive magic, from David. Mary's attempts to give an affirmative answer tormented Eleanor, since the only answer she could accept was: 'No, I'm not all right! I'm living in hell with a tyrannical madman, just as you did, my poor darling. On the other hand, I sincerely believe that the universe will save us, thanks to the awesome shamanic powers of the wounded healer that you truly are.'

For some reason Mary couldn't quite bring herself to say this, and yet there was still a troubling sisterhood between the two women. Mary recognized certain features of Eleanor's upbringing all too easily: the intense shyness, the all-important nanny, the diffident sense of self, the masochistic attraction to difficult men. Eleanor was the cautionary tale of these forces, a warning against the worthlessness of self-sacrifice when there was almost no self to sacrifice, of dealing with being lost by getting more lost. Above all, she was a baby, not a 'big baby' like so many adults, but a small baby perfectly preserved in the pickling jar of money, alcohol and fantasy.

Since that colourful day in Kew, neither of the boys had been taken to see their grandmother in her nursing home. Patrick stopped visiting her as well, after her excruciating flirtation with assisted suicide two years before. Only Mary persevered, sometimes with the scant dutiful reminder that Eleanor was, after all, her mother-in-law; sometimes with the more obscure conviction that Eleanor was out of balance with her family and that the work of redressing that balance must start straight away, whether Eleanor was able to participate or not. It was certainly strange, as the months wore on, to be talking into space, hoping that she was doing some good, while Eleanor stared ever more rigidly and blankly at the ceiling. And in the absence of any dialogue, she often ran aground on her contempt for Eleanor's failure to protect her child.

She could remember Eleanor describing the first few weeks after she returned from hospital with the infant Patrick. David was so tormented by his son's crying that he ordered her to take the noisy brat to the remotest room in the attic. Eleanor already felt exiled enough in David's beloved Cornwall, at the end of a headland overlooking an impenetrably wooded estuary, and she could hardly believe, as she was thrown out of her bedroom too suddenly to put on her slippers, or to collect a blanket for the baby, that there was a further exile available, a small cold room in the big cold house. For her the building was already sodden with melancholy horror. She had married David in the Truro registry office when she was heavily pregnant with their first child. Overestimating his medical skills, he had encouraged her to have the child at home. Without the incubator that she needed, Georgina died two days later. David sailed his boat out into the estuary, buried her at sea, and then disappeared for three days to get drunk. Eleanor stayed in bed, bleeding and abandoned, staring at the grey water through the bay window of her bedroom. After Georgina's death, she had refused to go to bed with David. One evening he punched her in the back of the knees as she was going upstairs. When she fell, he twisted her arm behind her back and raped her on the staircase. Just as she thought she was finally disgusted enough to leave him, she found that she was pregnant.

Up in the attic with the new rape-born baby in her arms, she felt hysterically unconfident. Looking at the narrow bed she was gripped by the fear that if they lay down on it together, she would roll over and asphyxiate him, and so she chose the wooden chair in the corner, next to the empty fireplace, and sat up all night, clutching him in her arms. During those nights in the wooden chair, she was sucked down into sleep again and again, and then woken abruptly by sensing the baby's body sliding down her nightdress towards the precipice of her knees. She would catch him at the last moment, terrified that his soft head was about to crash onto the hard floor; and yet unable to go to the bed they both longed for, in case she crushed him to death.

The days were a little better. The maternity nurse came in to help, the housekeeper bustled about in the kitchen, and with David out sailing and drinking, the house took on a superficially cheerful atmosphere. The three women fussed over Patrick and when Eleanor was resting back in her own bedroom she almost forgot about the dreadful nights; she almost forgot about the death of Georgina when she closed her eyes and could no longer see the stretch of grey water outside her window, and when she fed the baby from her breasts and they fell asleep together, she almost forgot about the violence that had brought him into the world.

But then one day, three weeks after they came back from hospital, David stayed behind. He was in a dangerous mood from the start; she could smell the brandy in his coffee and see the furious jealousy in his looks. By lunchtime, he had wounded everyone in the house with his cutting remarks, and all the women were anxious, feeling him pacing around, waiting for the chance to hurt and humiliate them. Nevertheless, they were surprised when he strode into the kitchen, carrying a battered leather bag and wearing a surgeon's ill-fitting green pyjamas. He ordered them to clear a space on the scrubbed oak table, unfolded a towel, took out a wooden case of surgical instruments from the bag and opened it next to the towel. He asked for a saucepan of boiling water, as if everything had already been agreed and everyone knew what was going on.

'What for?' said the housekeeper, the first to wake from the trance.

'To sterilize the instruments,' David answered in the tone of a man explaining something very obvious to someone very stupid. 'The time has come to perform a circumcision. Not, I assure you,' he added, as if to allay their innermost fears, 'for religious reasons,' he allowed himself a fleeting smile, 'but for medical ones.'

'You've been drinking,' Eleanor blurted out.

'Only a beaker of surgical spirit,' he quipped, a little giddy from the prospect of the operation; and then, no longer in the mood for fun, 'Bring me the boy.'

'Are you sure it's for the best?' asked the maternity nurse.

'Do not question my authority,' said David, throwing everything into it: the older man, the doctor, the employer, the centuries of command, but also the paralysing dart of his psychological presence, which made it seem life-threatening to oppose him.

His credentials as a murderer were well established in Eleanor's imagination. Late at night, when he was down to one listener, amongst the empty bottles and crushed cigars, David was fond of telling the story of an Indian pig-sticking hunt he had been on in the late nineteen-twenties. He was thrilled by the danger of galloping through the high grass with a lance, chasing a wild boar whose tusks could ruin a horse's legs, throw a rider to the ground and gore him to death. Impaling one of these fast, tough pigs was also a terrific pleasure, more involving than a long-distance kill. The only blemish on the expedition was that one of the party was bitten by a wild dog and developed the symptoms of rabies. Three days from the nearest hospital, it was already too late to help, and so the hunters decided to truss up their foaming and thrashing friend in one of the thick nets originally intended for transporting the bodies of the dead pigs, and to hoist him off the ground, tying the corners of the net to the branches of a big jacaranda tree. It was challenging, even for these hard men, to enjoy the sense of deep relaxation that follows a day of invigorating sport with this parcel of hydrophobic anguish dangling from a nearby tree. The row of lanterns down the dinner table, the quiet gleam of silver, the well-trained servants, the triumph of imposing civilization on the wild vastness of the Indian night, seemed to have been thrown into question. David could only just make out, against a background of screams, the splendid tale of Archie Montcrieff driving a pony and trap into the Viceroy's ballroom. Archie had worn an improvised toga and shouted obscenities in 'an outlandish kind of Cockney Latin', while the pony manured the dance floor. If his father hadn't been such a friend of the Viceroy's he might have had to resign his commission, but as it was, the viceroy admitted, privately of course, that Archie had raised his spirits during 'another damned dull dance'.

When the story was finished, David rose from the

table muttering, 'This noise is intolerable,' and went into his tent to fetch his pistol. He walked over to the rabies victim and shot him in the head. Returning to the dumbfounded table, he sat down with a 'feeling of absolute calm' and said, 'Much the kindest thing to do.' Gradually, the word spread around the table: much the kindest thing to do. Rich and powerful men, some of them quite high up in government, and one of them a judge, couldn't help agreeing with him. With the silencing of the screams and a few pints of whisky and soda, it became the general view by the end of the evening that David had done something exceptionally courageous. David would almost smile as he described how he had brought everyone at the table round, and then in a fit of piety, he would sometimes finish by saying that although at the time he had not yet set eyes on a copy of *Gray's Anatomy*, he really thought of that pistol shot as the beginning of his 'love affair with medicine'.

Eleanor felt obliged to hand over the baby to him in the kitchen in Cornwall. The baby screamed and screamed. Eleanor thought there must be dogs whimpering in their kennels a hundred miles away, the screams were so loud and high. All the women huddled together crying and begging David to stop and to be careful and to give the baby some local anaesthetic. They knew this was no operation, it was an attack by a furious old man on his son's genitals; but like the chorus in a play, they could only comment and wail, without being able to alter the action.

'I wanted to say, "You've already killed Georgina and now you want to kill Patrick,"' Eleanor told Mary, to show how bold she would have been if she had said anything at all. 'I wanted to call the police!'

Well, why didn't you? was all that Mary could think, but she said nothing about Eleanor saying nothing; she just nodded and went on being a good listener.

'It was like . . .' said Eleanor, 'it was like that Goya painting of Saturn devouring his son.' Brought up surrounded by great paintings, Eleanor had experienced a late-adolescent crush on the History of Art, rudely guillotined by her disinheritance, and replaced by a proclivity for bright dollops of optimistic symbolism. Nevertheless, she could still remember, when she was twenty, driving through Spain in her first car, and being shocked, on a visit to the Prado, by the black vision of those late Goyas.

Mary was struck by the comparison, because it was unusual for Eleanor to make that sort of connection, and also because she knew the painting well, and could easily visualize the gaping mouth, the staring eyes and the ragged white hair of the old god of melancholy, mad with jealousy and the fear of usurpation, as he fed on the bleeding corpse of his decapitated child. Watching Eleanor plead for exoneration made Mary realize that her mother-in-law could never have protected anyone else when she was so entranced by her own vulnerability, so desperate to be saved. Later in her marriage, Eleanor did manage to get police protection for herself. It was in Saint-Nazaire, just after she learned about her mother's death and, not yet knowing the content of the will, was expecting to get control of a world-class fortune. She had to fly to Rome later that morning for the funeral, and David sat opposite her at the breakfast table, brooding about the possible consequences of his wife's increased independence.

'You're looking forward to getting your hands on all that lovely money,' he said, walking round to her side of the table. She got up, sensing danger. 'But you're not going to,' he added, grabbing her and pressing his thumbs expertly into her throat, 'because I'm going to kill you.'

Almost unconscious, she had managed to knee him in the balls with all her remaining strength. In the reflex of pain, he let go long enough for her to slide across the table and bolt out of the house. He pursued her for a while, but the twenty-three-year age differ-ence took its toll on his tired body and she escaped into the woods. Convinced that he would follow by car, she struggled through the undergrowth to the local police station, and arrived scratched, bleeding and in tears. The two gendarmes who drove her back to the house stood guard over a proud and sulky David while she packed her bags for Rome. She left with relief, but without Patrick, who stayed behind with only the flimsy protection of yet another terri-fied nanny – they lasted, on average, about six weeks. Eleanor might have been out of reach, but once he had given the nanny a munificent day out, and sent Yvette home, David had the consolation of torturing his son without any interference from the gendarmerie.

In the end, Eleanor's betrayal of the maternal instinct that ruled Mary's own life formed an absolute barrier to the liking she could feel for her. She could remember her own sons at three weeks old: their hot silky heads burrowing their way back into the shelter of her body to soften the shock of being born. The thought of handing them over, before their skin could bear the roughness of wool, to be hacked at with knives by a cruel and sinister man required a level of treachery that blinded her imagination.

No doubt David had searched hard among the foolish and the meek to find a woman who could put up with his special tastes, but once his depravity was on full display, how could Eleanor escape the charge of colluding with a sadist and a paedophile? She had invited children from other families to spend their holidays in the South of France and, like Patrick, they had been raped and inducted into an underworld of shame and secrecy, backed by convincing threats of punishment and death. Just before her first stroke, Eleanor received a letter from one of those children, saying that after a lifetime of insomnia, self-harm, frigidity, promiscuity, perpetual anxiety and suicide attempts, she had started to lead a more normal life, thanks to seven years of therapy, and had finally been able to forgive Eleanor for not protecting her during the summer she stayed with the Melroses. When she showed the letter to Mary, Eleanor dwelt on the injustice of being made to feel guilty about a category of behaviour she had not even known existed, although it was going on in the bedroom next to hers.

And yet how ignorant could she really have been? The year before the arrival of the letter that so dis-

mayed Eleanor, Patrick had received a letter from
Sophie, an old au pair, who had heroically stayed
with the Melroses for more than two years, more
than twenty times the average endurance shown by
the parade of incredulous young foreign women who
passed through the house. In her letter, Sophie confessed to decades of guilt about the time she had spent
looking after Patrick. She used to hear screams down
the corridor of the house in Lacoste, and she knew
that Patrick was being tormented, not merely punished
or frustrated, but she was only nineteen at the time
and she hesitated to intervene. She also confessed that
she was terrified of David and, despite being genuinely
fond of Patrick and feeling some pity for Eleanor,
longed to get away from his grotesque family.

If Sophie knew that something was terribly wrong,
how could Eleanor not have known? It was common
enough to ignore what was seemingly impossible to
ignore, but Eleanor stuck to her blindness with un-
common tenacity. Through all her programmes of
self-discovery and shamanic healing, she avoided acknowledging her passion for avoidance. If she had
ever discovered her real 'power animals', Mary suspected they would have been the Three Monkeys:
See No Evil, Hear No Evil, Speak No Evil. Mary also

suspected that these grim vigilantes had been killed off by one of her strokes, flooding her all at once with the fragments of knowledge that she had kept sealed off from one another, like the cells of a secret organization. In a parody of wholeness, the fragments converged when it was too late to make them cohere.

Eleanor was entirely confined to the nursing home for the last two years of her life, rarely leaving her bed. For the first year, Mary went on assuming that at least one of the threads holding Eleanor to her tormented existence was concern for her family, and she continued to reassure her that they were well. Later, she began to see that what really trapped Eleanor was not the strength of her attachments, but rather their weakness: without anything substantial to 'let go' of, she was left with only the volatility of her guilt and confusion. Part of her was aching to die, but she could never find the time; there was no gap between the proliferating anxieties; the desire to die collided instantly with the dread of dying, which in turn gave birth to a renewed desire.

For the second year, Mary was largely silent. She went into the room and wished Eleanor well. What else was there to do?

The last time she had seen her mother-in-law was

two weeks ago. By then Eleanor had achieved a tranquillity indistinguishable from pure absence. Gaunt
and drawn, her face seemed incapable of any deliberate change. Mary could remember Eleanor telling
her, in one of those alienating confidential chats,
that she knew exactly when she was going to die. The
mysterious source of this information (Astrology?
Channelling? A morbid guru? A drumming session? A
prophetic dream?) was never unveiled, but the news
was delivered with the slightly boastful serenity of
pure fantasy. Mary felt that the certainty of death and
the uncertainty of both its timing and its meaning were
fundamental facts of life. Eleanor, on the other hand,
knew exactly when she was going to die and that her
death was not final. By the end, as far as Mary could
tell, this conviction had deserted Eleanor, along with
all the other features of her personality, as if a sand-
storm had raged through her, ripping away every sign
of comfort and leaving a smooth and sterile landscape
under a dry blank sky.

Still, Eleanor had died on Easter Sunday, and Mary
knew that nothing could have pleased her more. Or
would have pleased her more, had she known. Perhaps
she did know, even though her mind appeared to be
fixed in a realm removed from anything as mundane

as a calendar. Even then there was still no way of knowing whether that was the day she had been expecting to die.

Mary adjusted her position on the uncomfortable crematorium bench. Where was a convincing and practical theory of consciousness when you really needed it? She glanced back a few rows at Erasmus, but he appeared to have fallen asleep. As she turned back to the coffin a few feet in front of her, Mary's speculations collapsed abruptly. She found herself imagining, with a vividness she couldn't sustain while it was still going on, how it had felt for Eleanor during those two last brutal years, having her individuality annihilated, faculty by faculty, memory by memory.

Her eyes blurred with tears.

'Are you all right?' whispered Patrick, as he sat down next to her.

'I was thinking about your mother,' she said.

'A highly suitable choice,' Patrick murmured, in the voice of a sycophantic shopkeeper.

For some reason Mary started to laugh uncontrollably, and Patrick started laughing too, and they both had to bite their lower lips and keep their shoulders from shaking too wildly.

5

Hoping to master his fit of grief-stricken laughter, Patrick breathed out slowly and concentrated on the dull tension of waiting to begin. The organ sighed, as if bored of searching for a decent tune, and then meandered on resignedly. He must pull himself together: he was here to mourn his mother's death, a serious business.

There were various obstructions in his way. For a long time the feeling of madness brought on by the loss of his French home had made it impossible to get over his resentment of Eleanor. Without Saint-Nazaire, a primitive part of him was deprived of the imaginary care that had kept him sane as a child. He was certainly attached to the beauty of the place, but much more deeply to a secret protection that he dare not renounce in case it left him utterly destroyed. The shifting faces formed by the cracks, stains and hollows of the limestone mountain opposite the house used to keep him company. The line of pine trees along its ridge was like a column of soldiers coming to his rescue. There were hiding places where nobody had ever found him, and vine terraces to jump down, giving him the feeling he could fly when he had to flee. There was a dangerous well where he could drown rocks and clods of earth, without drowning himself. The most heroic connection of all was with the gecko that had taken custody of his soul in a moment of crisis and dashed out onto the roof, to safety and to exile. How could it ever find him again, if Patrick wasn't there any more?

On his last night in Saint-Nazaire there was a spectacular storm. Sheet lightning flickered behind ribbed banks of cloud, making the dark bowl of the valley tremble with light. At first, fat tropical raindrops dented the dusty ground, but soon enough, rivulets guttered down the steep paths, and little waterfalls flowed from step to step. Patrick wandered outside into the warm heavy rain, feeling mad. He knew that he had to end his magical contract with this land-scape, but the electric air and the violent protest of the storm renewed the archaic mentality of a child, as if the same thick piano wires, hammered by thunder and pelting rain, ran through his body and the land. With water streaming down his face there was no need for tears, no need to scream with the sky cracking overhead. He stood in the drive, among the milky puddles and the murmur of new steams and the smell of the wet rosemary, until he sank to the ground, weighed down by what he was unable to give up, and sat motionless in the gravel and the mud. Forked lightning landed like antlers on the limestone mountain. In that sudden flash, he made out a shape on the ground between him and the wall that ran along the edge of the drive. Concentrating in the murky light, he saw that a toad had ventured out into the watery world beyond the laurel bushes, where Patrick imagined it had been waiting all summer for the rain, and was now resting gratefully on a bar of muddy ground between two puddles. They sat in front of each other, perfectly still.

Patrick pictured the white corpses of the toads he used to see each spring, at the bottom of the stone pools. Around their spent bodies, hundreds of soft black tadpoles clung to the grey-green algae on the walls, or wriggled across the open pond, or overflowed into the runnels that carried the water from pool to pool, between the source and the stream in the crease of the valley. Some of the tadpoles slipped limply down the slope; others swam frantically against the current. Robert and Thomas spent hours each Easter holiday, removing the little dams that formed over-night, and, when the covered part of the channel was blocked and the grass around the lower pond flooded, airlifting the stranded tadpoles in their cupped hands. Patrick could remember doing the same thing as a child, and the sense of giant compassion that he used to feel as he released them back into the safety of the pond through his flooding fingers.

In those days there had been a chorus of frogs during the spring nights, and during the day, sitting on the lily pads in the crescent pond, bullfrogs blowing their insides out like bubble gum; but in the system of imaginary protection that the land used to allow him, it was the lucky tree frogs that really counted. If only he could touch one of them, everything would be all right. They were hard to find. The round suckers on the tips of their feet meant that they could hang anywhere in the tree, camouflaged by the bright green of a new leaf or an unripe fig. When he did see one of these tiny frogs, fixed to the smooth grey bark, its brilliant skin stretched over a sharp skeleton, it looked to him like pulsing jewellery. He would reach out his index finger and touch it lightly for good luck. It might have only happened once, but he had thought about it a thousand times.

Remembering that charged and tentative gesture, he now looked with some scepticism at the warty head of the sodden toad in front of him. At the same time, he remembered his A-level Arden edition of *King Lear* with its footnote about the jewel in the head of the toad, the emblem of the treasure hidden in the midst of ugly, muddy, repulsive experience. One day he would live without superstition, but not yet. He reached out and touched the head of the toad. He felt some of the same awe he had felt as a child, but the resurgence of what he was about to lose gave the feeling a self-cancelling intensity. The mad fusion of mythologies created an excess of meaning that might at any moment flip into a world with no meaning at all. He drew away and, like someone returning to the familiar compromises of his city flat after a long exotic journey, recognized that he was a middle-aged man, sitting eccentrically in his muddy driveway in the middle of a thunderstorm, trying to communicate with a toad. He got up stiffly and slouched back to the house, feeling realistically miserable, but still kicking the puddles in defiance of his useless maturity.

Eleanor had given Saint-Nazaire away, but at least she had provided it in the first place, if only as a massive substitute for herself, a motherland that was there to cover for her incapacities. In a sense its loveliness was a decoy, the branches of almond blossom reaching into a cloudless sky, the unopened irises, like paintbrushes dipped in blue, the clear amber resin bleeding from the gunmetal bark of the cherry trees – all of that was a decoy, he must stop thinking about it. A child's need for protection would have assembled a system out of whatever materials came to hand, however ritual or bizarre. It might have been a spider in a broom cupboard, or the appearance of a neighbour across the well of a block of flats, or the number of red cars between the front door and the school gates, that took on the burden of love and reassurance. In his case, it had been a hillside in France. His home had stretched from the dark pinewood at the top of the slope, all the way to the pale bamboo that grew beside the stream at its foot. In between were terraces where vine shoots burst from twisted stumps that spent the winter looking like rusted iron, and olive trees rushed from green to grey and grey to green in the combing wind. Halfway down the slope were the cluster of houses and cypresses and the network of pools where he had experienced the most horror and negotiated the most far-fetched reprieves. Even the steep mountainside opposite the house was colonized by his imagination, and not only with the army of trees marching along its crest. Later on, its rejection of human encroachment became an image of his own less reliable aloofness.

Nobody could spend their whole life in a place without missing it when they left. Pathetic fallacies, projections, substitutions and displacements were part of the inevitable traffic between any mind and its habitual surroundings, but the pathological intensity he had brought to these operations made it vital for him to see through them. What would it be like to live without consolation, or the desire for consolation? He would never find out, unless he uprooted the consolatory system that had started on the hillside at Saint-Nazaire and then spread to every medicine cabinet, bed and bottle he had come across since; substitutes substituting for substitutes: the system was always more fundamental than its contents, and the mental act more fundamental still. What if memories were just memories, without any consolatory or persecutory power? Would they exist at all, or was it always emotional pressure that summoned images from what was potentially all of experience so far? Even if that was the case, there must be better librarians than panic, resentment and dismembering nostalgia to search among the dim and crowded stacks.

Whereas ordinary generosity came from a desire to give something to someone, Eleanor's philanthropy had come from a desire to give everything to anyone. The sources of the compulsion were complex. There was the repetition syndrome of a disinherited daughter; there was a rejection of the materialism and snobbery of her mother's world; and there was the basic shame at having any money at all, an unconscious drive to make her net worth and her self-worth converge in a perfect zero; but apart from all these negative forces, there was also the inspiring precedent of her great-aunt Virginia Jonson. With a rare enthusiasm for an ancestor, Eleanor used to tell Patrick all about the heroic scale of Virginia's charitable works; how she made so much difference to so many lives, showing that ardent selflessness which is often more stubborn than open egotism.

Virginia had already lost two sons when her husband died in 1901. Over the next twenty-five years she demolished half the Jonson fortune with her mournful philanthropy. In 1903 she endowed the Thomas

J. Jonson Memorial Fund with twenty million dollars and in her will with another twenty-five million, at a time when these were sums of a rare vastness, rather than the typical Christmas bonus of a mediocre hedge-fund manager. She also collected paintings by Titian, Rubens, Van Dyck, Rembrandt, Tintoretto, Bronzino, Lorenzo di Credi, Murillo, Velasquez, Hals, Le Brun, Gainsborough, Romney and Botticelli, and donated them to the Jonson Wing of the Cleveland Museum of Art. This cultural legacy was what interested Eleanor least, perhaps because it resembled too closely the private acquisitive frenzy taking place in her own branch of the Jonson family. What she really admired were Virginia's Good Works, the hospitals and YMCAs she built, and above all, the new town she created on a four-hundred-acre site, in the hope of clearing Cleveland's slums by giving ideal housing to the poor. It was named Friendship, after her summer place in Newport. When it was completed in 1926, Virginia addressed a 'Greeting' to its first residents in the *Friendship Messenger*.

> Good morning. Is the sun a little brighter, there in Friendship? Is the air a little fresher? Is your home a little sweeter? Is your house-work somewhat easier? And the children – do

you feel safer about them? Are their faces a little ruddier; are their legs a little sturdier? Do they laugh and play a lot louder in Friendship? Then I am content.

To Eleanor, there had been something deeply moving about this Queen Victoria of Ohio, a little woman with a puffy white face, always dressed in black, always reclusive, seeking no personal glory for her charitable acts, driven by deep religious convictions, still naming streets and buildings after her dead sons right up to the end – her Albert had his Avenue and her Sheldon had his Close in the safer, child-friendly precincts of Friendship.

At the same time, the coolness of relations between the Jonson sisters and their Aunt Virginia showed that in the opinion of her nieces she had not struck the right balance between the civic-minded and the family-minded. If anyone was going to give away Jonson money, the sisters felt that it should be them, rather than the daughter of a penniless clergyman who had married their uncle Thomas. They were each left a hundred thousand dollars in Virginia's will. Even her friends did better. She endowed a Trust with two and a half million dollars to provide annuities for sixty-nine friends for the rest of their lives. Patrick suspected that Virginia's talent for annoying Eleanor's mother and her aunts was the unacknowledged source of Eleanor's admiration for her great-aunt. She and Virginia stood apart from the dynastic ambitions of wealth. For them, money was a trust from God that must be used to do good in the world. Patrick hoped that during her frantic silence in the nursing home, Eleanor had been dreaming, at least some of the time, of the place she might occupy next to the great Jonson philanthropist who had Gone Before.

Virginia's meanness to the Jonson Sisters was no doubt underpinned by the knowledge that her brother-in-law would leave each of them with a huge fortune.

Nevertheless, by their generation, the thrill of being rich was already shadowed by the shocks of disinheritance and the ironies of philanthropy. The 1929 Crash came two years after Virginia's death. The poor became destitute, and the white middle classes, who were much poorer than they used to be, fled the inner city for the half-timbered cosiness of Friendship, even though Virginia had built it in memory of a husband who was 'a friend to the Negro race'.

Eleanor's friendship was with something altogether vaguer than the Negro race. 'Friend to the neo-shamanic revival of the Celtic Twilight' seemed less likely to yield concrete social progress. During Patrick's childhood, her charitable focus had resembled Virginia's Good Works much more closely, except that it was devoted overwhelmingly to children. He had often been left alone with his father while Eleanor went to a committee meeting of the Save the Children Fund. The absolute banishment of irony from Eleanor's earnest persona created a black market for the blind sarcasm of her actions. Later, it was Father Tortelli and his Neapolitan street urchins who were the targets of her evasive charity. Patrick could not help thinking that this passion for saving all the children of the world was an unconscious admission that she could not save her own child. Poor Eleanor, how frightened she must have been. Patrick suddenly wanted to protect her.

When Patrick's childhood had ended and the inarticulate echoes of her own childhood faded, Eleanor stopped supporting children's charities, and embarked on the second adolescence of her New Age quest. She showed the same genius for generalization that had characterized her rescue of children, except that her identity crisis was not merely global, but interplanetary and cosmic as well, without sinking one millimetre into the resistant bedrock of self-knowledge. No stranger to 'the energy of the universe', she remained a stranger to herself. Patrick could not pretend that he would have applauded any charitable gift involving all his mother's property, but once that became inevitable, it was a further pity that it had all gone to the Transpersonal Foundation.

Aunt Virginia would not have approved either. She wanted to bring real benefits to fellow human beings. Her influence on Eleanor had been indirect but strong and, like all the other strong influences, matriarchal. The Jonson men sometimes seemed to Patrick like those diminutive male spiders that quickly discharge their only important responsibility before being eaten by the much larger females. The founder's two sons left two widows: Virginia, the widow of good works, and Eleanor's grandmother, the widow of good marriages, whose second marriage to the son of an English earl launched her three daughters on their dazzling social and matrimonial careers. Patrick knew that Nancy had been intending to write a book about the Jonsons for the last twenty years. Without any tiresome show of false modesty, she had said to him, 'I mean, it would be much better than Henry James and Edith Wharton and those sort of people, because it *really* happened.'

Men who married Jonson women didn't fare much

better than the founder's sons. Eleanor's father and her uncle Vladimir were both alcoholics, emasculated by getting the heiress they thought they wanted. They ended up sitting together in White's, nursing their wounds over a luxurious drink; divorced, discarded, cut off from their children. Eleanor was brought up wondering how an heiress could avoid destroying the man she married, unless he was already too corrupt to be destroyed, or rich enough to be immune. She had chosen from the first category in marrying David, and yet his malice and pride, which were impressive enough to begin with, were still magnified by the humiliation of depending on his wife's money.

Patrick was not one of the Jonson castrati by marriage, but he knew what it was to be born into a matriarchal world, given money by a grandmother he scarcely knew, and cut off by a mother who still expected him to look after her. The psychological impact of these powerful women, generous from an impersonal distance, treacherous up close, had furnished him with one basic model of what a woman should look like and how she would in fact turn out to be. The object of desire generated by this combination was the Hiso Bitch – Hiso was an acronym for high society invented by a Japanese friend of his. The

Hiso Bitch had to be a reincarnation of a Jonson Sister: glamorous, intensely social, infinitely rich in the pursuit of pleasure, embedded among beautiful possessions. As if this was not enough (as if this was not too much) she also had to be sexually voracious and morally disoriented. His first girlfriend had been an embryonic version of the type. He still thought sometimes about kneeling in front of her, in the pool of light from the reading lamp, the shining folds of her black silk pyjamas gathered between her splayed legs, a trickle of blood running down her proffered arm, the gasp of pleasure, whispering, 'Too much too much,' the film of sweat on her angular face, the syringe in his hand, her first fix of cocaine. He did his best to addict her, but she was a vampire of a different sort, feeding off the despairing obsession of the men who surrounded her, draining ever more socially assured admirers in the hope of acquiring their sense of belonging, even as she trivialized it in their eyes by making herself seem the only thing worth having and then walking away.

In his early thirties his compulsive search for disappointment brought him Inez, the Sistine Chapel of the Hiso Bitch. She insisted that every one of her cartload of lovers was exclusive to her, a condition she failed to secure from her husband, but successfully extorted from Patrick, who left the relatively sane and generous woman he was living with in order to plunge into the hungry vacuum of Inez's love. Her absolute indifference to the feelings of her lovers made her sexual receptiveness into a kind of free-fall. In the end the cliff he fell off was as flat as the one Gloucester was made to leap off by his devoted son: a cliff of blindness and guilt and imagination, with no beetling rocks at its base. But she did not know that and neither did he.

With her curling blonde hair and her slender limbs and her beautiful clothes, Inez was alluring in an obvious way, and yet it was easy enough to see that her slightly protruding blue eyes were blank screens of self-love on which a small selection of fake emotions was allowed to flicker. She made rather haphazard impersonations of someone who has relationships with others. Based on the gossip of her courtiers, a diet of Hollywood movies and the projection of her own cunning calculations, these guesses might be sentimental or nasty, but were always vulgar and melodramatic. Since she hadn't the least interest in the answer, she was inclined to ask, 'How *are* you?' with great gravity, at least half a dozen times. She was often exhausted by the thought of how generous she was, whereas the exhaustion really stemmed from the strain of not giving away anything at all. 'I'm going to buy six thoroughbred Arab stallions for the Queen of Spain's birthday,' she announced one day. 'Don't you think it's a good idea?'

'Is six enough?' asked Patrick.

'You don't think six is enough? Do you have any idea how much they cost?'

He was amazed when she did buy the horses, less surprised when she kept them for herself and bored when she sold them back to the man she had bought them from. However maddening she was as a friend, it was in the cut and thrust of romance that her talents excelled.

'I've never felt this way before,' she would say with troubled profundity. 'I don't think anybody has really understood me until now. Do you know that? Do you know how important you are to me?' Tears would well up in her eyes as she hardly dared to whisper, 'I don't think I've ever felt at home until now,' nestling in his strong, manly arms.

Soon afterwards he would be left waiting for days in some foreign hotel where Inez never bothered to show up. Her social secretary would call twice a day to say that she had been delayed but was really on her way now. Inez knew that this tantalizing absence was the most efficient way to ensure that he would think of nothing but her, while leaving her free to do the same thing at a safe distance. His mind might wander almost anywhere if she was lying in his arms talking nonsense, whereas if he was nailed to the telephone, haemorrhaging money and abandoning all his other responsibilities, he was bound to think of her constantly. When they did eventually meet up, she would hurry to point out how unbearable it had all been for her, ruthlessly monopolizing the suffering generated by her endlessly collapsing plans.

Why would anyone allow himself to be annihilated by such shallowness, unless a buried image of a careless woman was longing for outward form? Lateness, let-down, longing for the unobtainable: these were the mechanisms that turned a powerful matriarchal stimulant into a powerful maternal depressant. Bewildering lateness, especially, took him directly into an early despair, waiting in vain on the stairs for his mother to come, terrified that she was dead.

Patrick suddenly experienced these old emotions as a physical oppression. He ran his fingers along the inside of his collar to make sure that it was not concealing a tightening noose. He couldn't bear the lure of disappointment any longer, or for that matter the lure of consolation, its Siamese twin. He must somehow get beyond both of them, but first he had to mourn his mother. In a sense he had been missing her all his life. It was not the end of closeness but the end of the longing for closeness that he had to mourn. How futile his longing must have been for him to disperse himself into the land at Saint-Nazaire. If he tried to imagine anything deeper than his old home, he just pictured himself standing there, straining to see something elusive, shielding his eyes to watch a dragonfly dip into the burning water at noon, or starlings twisting against the setting sun.

He could now see that the loss of Saint-Nazaire was not an obstacle to mourning his mother but the only possible means to do so. Letting go of the imaginary world he had put in her place released him from that futile longing and took him into a deeper grief. He was free to imagine how terrified Eleanor must have been, for a woman of such good intentions, to have abandoned her desire to love him, which he did not doubt, and be compelled to pass on so much fear and panic instead. At last he could begin to mourn her for herself, for the tragic person she had been.

6

Patrick had little idea what to expect from the ceremony. He had been on a business trip to America at the time of his mother's death and pleaded the impossibility of preparing anything to say or read, leaving Mary to take over the arrangements. He had only arrived back from New York yesterday, just in time to go to Bunyon's funeral parlour, and now that he was sitting in a pew next to Mary, picking up the order of service for the first time, he realized how unready he was for this exploration of his mother's confusing life. On the front of the little booklet was a photograph of Eleanor in the sixties, throwing her arms out as if to embrace the world, her dark glasses firmly on and no breathalyser test results available. He hesitated to look inside; this was the muddle, the pile-up of fact and feeling he had been trying to outmanoeuvre since the end of Eleanor's flirtation with assisted suicide two years ago. She had died as a person before her body died, and he had tried to pretend that her life was over before it really was, but no amount of anticipation could cheat the demands of an actual death, and now, with a combination of embarrassment and fear and evasiveness, he leant forward and slipped the order of service back onto the shelf in front of him. He would find out what was in it soon enough.

He had gone to America after receiving a letter from Brown and Stone LLP, the lawyers for the John J. Jonson Corporation, known affectionately as 'Triple J'. They had been informed by 'the family' – Patrick now suspected that it was Henry who had told them – that Eleanor Melrose was incompetent to administer her own affairs, and since she was the beneficiary of a trust created by her grandfather, of which Patrick was the ultimate beneficiary, measures should be taken to procure him a U.S. power of attorney in order to administer the money on his mother's behalf. All this was news to Patrick and he was freshly astonished by his mother's capacity for secrecy. In his amazement he failed to ask how much the trust contained and he got onto the plane to New York not knowing whether he would be put in charge of twenty thousand dollars or two hundred thousand.

Joe Rich and Peter Zirkovsky met him in one of the smaller oval-tabled, glass-sided conference rooms of Brown and Stone's offices on Lexington Avenue. Instead of the sulphurous yellow legal pads he was expecting, he found lined cream paper with the name of the firm printed elegantly on the top of each page. An assistant photocopied Patrick's passport, while Joe examined the doctor's letter testifying to Eleanor's incapacity.

'I had no idea about this trust,' said Patrick.

'Your mother must have been keeping it as a nice surprise,' said Peter with a big lazy smile.

'It might be that,' said Patrick tolerantly. 'Where does the income go?'

'Currently we're sending it to . . .' Peter flicked over a sheet of paper, 'the Association Transpersonel at the Banque Populaire de la Côte d'Azur in Lacoste, France.'

'Well, you can stop that straight away,' said Patrick.

'Whoa, slow down,' said Joe. 'We're going to have to get you a power of attorney first.'

'That's why she didn't tell me about it,' said

Patrick, 'because she's continuing to subsidize her pet charity in France while I pay for her nursing-home fees in London.'

'She may have lost her competence before she had a chance to change the instructions,' said Peter, who seemed determined to furnish Patrick with a loving mother.

'This letter is fine,' said Joe. 'We're going to have to get you to sign some documents and get them notarized.'

'How much money are we talking about?' asked Patrick.

'It's not a large Jonson trust and it's suffered in the recent stock-market corrections,' said Joe.

'Let's hope it behaves incorrigibly from now on,' said Patrick.

'The latest valuation we have,' said Peter, glancing down at his notes, 'is two point three million dollars, with an estimated income of eighty thousand.'

'Oh, well, still a useful sum,' said Patrick, trying to sound slightly disappointed.

'Enough to buy a country cottage!' said Peter in an absurd impersonation of an English accent. 'I gather house prices are pretty crazy over there.'

'Enough to buy a second room,' said Patrick,

eliciting a polite guffaw from Peter, although Patrick could in fact think of nothing he wanted more than to separate the bed from the sit.

Walking down Lexington Avenue towards his hotel in Gramercy Park, Patrick began adjusting to his strange good fortune. The long arm of his great-grandfather, who had died more than half a century before Patrick was born, was going to pluck him out of his cramped living quarters and get him into a place where there might be room for his children to stay and his friends to visit. In the meantime it would pay for his mother's nursing home. It was puzzling to think that this complete stranger was going to have such a powerful influence on his life. Even his benefactor had inherited his money. It had been his father who had founded the Jonson Candle Company in Cleveland, in 1832. By 1845 it was one of the most profitable candle companies in the country. Patrick could remember reading the founder's uninspiring explanation for his success: 'We had a new process of distilling cheap greases. Our competitors were using costly tallow and lard. Candles were high and our profits were large for a number of years.' Later, the candle factory diversified into paraffin, oil treatment and hardening processes, and developed a patented compound that became an indispensable ingredient in dry cleaning around the world. The Jonsons also bought buildings and building sites in San Francisco, Denver, Kansas City, Toledo, Indianapolis, Chicago, New York, Trinidad and Puerto Rico, but the original fortune rested on the hard-headedness of the founder who had 'died on the job', falling through a hatchway in one of his own factories, and also on those 'cheap greases' which were still lubricating the life of one of his descendants a hundred and seventy years after their discovery.

John J. Jonson, Jr., Eleanor's grandfather, was already sixty by the time he finally married. He had been travelling the world in the service of his family's burgeoning business, and was only recalled from China by the death of his nephew Sheldon in a sledging accident at St Paul's School. His eldest nephew, Albert, had already died from pneumonia at Harvard the year before. There were no heirs to the Jonson fortune and Sheldon's grieving father, Thomas, told his brother it was his duty to marry. John accepted his fate and, after a brief courtship of a general's daughter, got married and moved to New York. He fathered three daughters in rapid succession, and then dropped dead, but not before creating a multitude of trusts, one of which was meandering its way down to Patrick, as he had discovered that afternoon.

What did this long-range goodwill mean, and what did it say about the social contract that allowed a rich man to free all of his descendents from the need to work over the course of almost two centuries? There was something disreputable about being saved by increasingly remote ancestors. When he had exhausted the money given to him by a grandmother he scarcely knew, money arrived from a great-grandfather he could never have known. He could feel only an abstract gratitude towards a man whose face he would not have been able to pick out from a heap of sepia daguerreotypes. The ironies of the dynastic drive were just as great as the philanthropic ironies generated by Eleanor, or her great-aunt Virginia. No doubt his grandmother and his great-grandfather had hoped to empower a senator, enrich a great art collection or encourage a dazzling marriage, but in the end they had mainly subsidized idleness, drunkenness, treachery and divorce. Were the ironies of taxation any better: raising money for schools and hospitals and roads and bridges, and spending it on blowing up schools and hospitals and roads and bridges in self-defeating wars?

It was hard to choose between these variously absurd methods of transferring wealth, but just for now he was going to cave in to the pleasure of having benefited from this particular form of American capitalism. Only in a country free from the funnelling of primogeniture and the levelling of égalité could the fifth generation of a family still be receiving parcels of wealth from a fortune that had essentially been made in the 1830s. His pleasure coexisted peacefully with his disapproval, as he walked into his dim and scented hotel, which resembled the film set of an expensive Spanish brothel, with the room numbers sewn into the carpet, on the assumption that the guests were on all fours after some kind of near overdose and could no longer find their rooms as they crawled down the obscure corridors.

The phone was ringing when he arrived in the velvet jewel box of his room, bathed in the murky urine light of parchment lampshades and presumptive hangover. He groped his way to the bedside table, clipping his shin on the bowed legs of a chair designed to resemble the virile effeminacy of a matador's jacket, with immense epaulettes jutting out proudly from the top of its stiff back.

'Fuck,' he said as he answered the phone.

'Are you all right?' said Mary.

'Oh, hi, sorry, it's you. I just got impaled on this fucking matador chair. I can't see anything in this hotel. They ought to hand out miner's helmets at the reception.'

'Listen, I've got some bad news.' She paused.

Patrick lay back on the pillows with a clear intuition of what she was going to say.

'Eleanor died last night. I'm sorry.'

'What a relief,' said Patrick defiantly. 'Amongst other things . . .'

'Yes, other things as well,' said Mary and she gave the impression of accepting them all in advance.

They agreed to talk in the morning. Patrick had a fervent desire to be left alone matched only by his fervent desire not to be left alone. He opened the minibar and sat on the floor cross-legged, staring at the wall of miniatures on the inside of the door, shining in the dazzling light of the little white fridge. On shelves next to the tumblers and wine glasses were chocolates, jellybeans, salted nuts, treats and bribes for tired bodies and discontented children. He closed the fridge and closed the cupboard door and climbed carefully onto the red velvet sofa, avoiding the matador chair as best he could.

He must try not to forget that only a year ago hallucinations had been crashing into his helpless mind like missiles into a besieged city. He lay down on the sofa, clutching a heavily embroidered cushion to his already aching stomach, and slipped effortlessly into the delirious mentality of his little room in the Priory. He remembered how he used to hear the scratch of a metal nib, or the flutter of moth wings on a screen door, or the swish of a carving knife being sharpened, or the pebble clatter of a retreating wave, as if they were in the same room with him, or rather as if he was in the same place as them. There was a broken rock streaked with the hectic glitter of quartz that quite often lay at the foot of his bed. Blue lobsters explored the edges of the skirting board with their sensitive antennae. Sometimes it was whole scenes that took him over. He would picture, for instance, brake lights streaming across a wet road, the smoky interior of a car, the throb of familiar music, a swollen drop of water rushing down the windscreen, consuming the other drops in its path, and feel that this atmosphere was the deepest thing he had ever known. The absence of narrative in these compulsory waking dreams ushered in a more secretive sense of connection. Instead of trudging across the desert floor of ordinary succession, he was plunged into an oceanic night lit by isolated flares of bioluminescence. He surfaced from these states, unable to imagine how he could describe their haunting power to his Depression Group and longing for his breakfast oxazepam.

He could have all that back with a few months of hard drinking, not just the quicksilver swamps of early withdrawal with their poisonous, fugitive, shattering reflections, and the discreet delirium of the next two weeks, but all the group therapy as well. He could still remember, on his third day in the Alcohol and Addiction Group, wanting to dive out of the window when an old-timer had dropped in to share his experience, strength and hope with the trembling foals of early recovery. A well-groomed ex-meths drinker, with white hair and a smoker's orange fingers, he had quoted the wisdom of an even older-timer who was 'in the rooms' when he first 'came round': 'Fear knocked at the door!' (Pause) 'Courage answered the door!' (Pause) 'And there was nobody there!' (Long pause). He could also have more of the Scottish moderator from the Depression Group, with his cute mnemonic for the power of projection: 'you've got what you spot and you spot what you've got'. And then there were the 'rock bottoms' of the other patients to reconsider, the man who woke next to a girlfriend he couldn't remember slashing with a kitchen knife the night before; the weekend guest surrounded by the hand-painted wallpaper he couldn't remember smearing with excrement; the woman whose arm was amputated when the syringe she picked up from the concrete floor of a friend's flat turned out to be infected with a flesh-eating superbug; the mother who abandoned her terrified children in a remote holiday cottage in order to return to her dealer in London and countless other stories of less demonstrative despair – moments of shame that precipitated 'moments of clarity' in the pilgrim's progress of recovery.

All in all, the minibar was out. His month in the Priory had worked. He knew as deeply as he knew anything that sedation was the prelude to anxiety, stimulation the prelude to exhaustion and consolation the prelude to disappointment, and so he lay on the red velvet sofa and did nothing to distract himself from the news of his mother's death. He stayed awake through the night feeling unconvincingly numb. At five in the morning, when he calculated that Mary would

EDWARD ST. AUBYN

be back from the school run in London, he called
her flat and they agreed that she would take over the
arrangements for the funeral.

The organ fell silent, interrupting Patrick's daydream.
He picked up the booklet again from the narrow
shelf in front of him, but before he had time to look
inside, music burst out from the speakers in the corners of the room. He recognized the song just before
the deep black cheerful voice rang out over the crematorium.

> *Oh, I got plenty o' nuthin',*
> *An' nuthin's plenty fo' me.*
> *I got no car, got no mule, I got no misery.*
> *De folks wid plenty o' plenty*
> *Got a lock on dey door,*
> *'Fraid somebody's a-goin' to rob 'em*
> *While dey's out a-makin' more.*
> *What for?*

Patrick looked round and smiled mischievously at
Mary. She smiled back. He suddenly felt irrationally
guilty that he hadn't yet told her about the trust, as if
he were no longer entitled to enjoy the song, now that
he didn't have quite as much *nuthin'* as before. *More. /*

What for? was a rhyme that deserved to be made more often.

> *Oh, I got plenty o' nuthin',*
> *An' nuthin's plenty fo' me.*
> *I got de sun, got de moon,*
> *Got de deep blue sea.*
> *De folks wid plenty o' plenty,*
> *Got to pray all de day.*
> *Seems wid plenty you sure got to worry*
> *How to keep de debble away,*
> *A-way.*

Patrick was entertained by Porgy's insistence on the sinfulness of riches. He felt that Eleanor and aunt Virginia would have approved. After all, before they became masters of the universe, usurers were consigned to the seventh circle of Hell. Under a rain of fire, their perpetually restless hands were a punishment for hands that had made nothing useful or good in their lifetime, just exploited the labour of others. Even from the less breezy position of being one of the *folks wid plenty o' plenty*, and at the cost of buying into the fantasy that folks with *plenty o' nuttin'* didn't also have to worry about keeping the *Debble* away, Eleanor would have endorsed Porgy's views.

Patrick renewed his concentration for the final part of the song.

> *Never one to strive*
> *To be good, to be bad—*
> *What the hell! I is glad*
> *I's alive!*
>
> *Oh, I got plenty o' nuthin',*
> *An' nuthin's plenty fo' me.*
> *I got my gal, got my song,*
> *Got Hebben de whole day long.*
> *(No use complainin'!)*
> *Got my gal, got my Lawd, got my song!*

'Great choice,' Patrick whispered to Mary with a grateful nod. He picked up the order of service again, finally ready to look inside.

7

How nauseating, thought Nicholas, a Jew being sentimental on behalf of a Negro: you lucky fellows, you've
got plenty o' nuthin', whereas we're weighed down
with all this international capital and these wretched
Broadway musical hits. When an idea is floundering,
Nicholas said to himself, practising for later, songwrit-
ers always wheel out the celestial bodies. *De things
dat I prize, / Like de stars in de skies, / All are free.*
No surprises there – one couldn't expect to get much
rent from a hydrogen bomb several million light-years
away. It was hard enough persuading a merchant
banker to cough up a decent rent for one's lovely
Grade II listed Queen Anne dower house in Shrop-
shire, without asking him to drive to the moon for
the weekend. Talk about too far from London, and
nothing to do when one got there, except bounce

around while the oxygen runs out. There was such a thing as the way of the world. Sixty per cent of the *Titanic*'s first-class passengers survived; twenty-five per cent of the second-class passengers, and no one from steerage. That was the way of the world. 'Sure is grateful, boss,' simpered Nicholas under his breath, 'I got de deep blue sea.'

Oh, God, what was going on now? The ghastly 'Spiritual Tool Box' was going up to the lectern. He could hardly bear it. What was he doing here? In the end, he was just as sentimental as silly old Ira Gershwin. He had come for David Melrose. In many ways David had been an obscure failure, but his presence had possessed a rare and precious quality: pure contempt. He bestrode middle-class morality like a colossus. Other people laboured through the odd bigoted remark, but David had embodied an absolute disdain for the opinion of the world. One could only do one's best to keep up the tradition.

For Erasmus the most interesting lines were undoubtedly, *Never one to strive / To be good, to be bad— / What the hell! I is glad / I's alive!* Nietzsche was there, of course, and Rousseau (inevitably), but also the Diamond Sutra. Porgy was unlikely to have read any of them.

Nevertheless, it was legitimate to think in terms of the pervasive influence of a certain family of ideas, of non-striving and of a natural state that preceded rule-based morality and in some sense made it redundant. Maybe he could see Mary after the funeral. She had always been so receptive. He sometimes thought about that.

Thank goodness there were people who were happy with nothing, thought Julia, so that people like her (and everyone else she had ever met), could have *more*. It was virtually impossible to think of a sentence that made a positive use of that dreadful word 'enough', let alone one that started raving about 'nothing'. Still, the song was rather perfect for Patrick's dotty mother, as well as being an upbeat disinheritance anthem. Hats off to Mary, as usual. Julia sighed with admiration. She assumed that Patrick had been feeling too 'mad' to do anything practical, and that Mother Mary had been asked to step in.

Really, thought Nancy, it was too ridiculous to turn to the Gershwin brothers when one's own godfather was the divine Cole Porter. Why had Mummy wasted him on indifferent Eleanor when Nancy, who really appreciated his glamour and wit, might have had him all to herself? Not that *Porgy and Bess* didn't have its glamorous side. She had gone to a big New York opening with Hansie and Dinkie Guttenburg and had the best time ever, going backstage to congratulate everybody. The real stars weren't at all overawed by meeting a ferociously handsome German prince with a severe stutter, but you could tell that some of the little chorus girls didn't know whether to curtsy, start a revolution, or poison his wife. She would definitely include that scene in her book, it was such a coming together of everything fun, unlike this drab funeral. Really, Eleanor was letting the family down and letting herself down as well.

Annette was stunned, as she walked down the aisle towards the lectern, by the appropriateness, the serendipity and the synchronicity of that wonderful, spiritual song. Only yesterday she had been sitting with Seamus at their favourite power point on the terrace at Saint-Nazaire (actually they had decided that it was the heart chakra of the entire property, which made perfect sense when you thought about it), celebrating Eleanor's unique gifts with a glass of red wine, and Seamus had mentioned her incredibly strong connection with the African-American people. He had been privileged to be present at several of Eleanor's past-life regressions and it turned out that she had been a runaway slave during the American Civil War, trying to make her way to the abolitionist North with a young baby in her arms. She'd had the most terrible time of it, apparently, only travelling at night, in the dead of winter, hiding in ditches and living in fear for her life. And now, the very next day, at Eleanor's funeral, a man who was obviously the descendant of a slave was singing those marvellous lyrics. Perhaps – Annette almost came to a halt, overwhelmed by further horizons of magical coincidence – perhaps he was the very baby Eleanor had carried to freedom through the ditches and the night, grown into a splendid man with a deep and resonant voice. It was almost unbearably beautiful, but she had a task to perform and with a regretful tug she extracted herself from the amazing dimension to which her train of thought had transported her, and stood squarely at the lectern, unfolding the pages she had been carrying in the pocket of her dress. She fingered the amber necklace she had bought at the Mother Meera gift shop when she had gone for *darshan* with the avatar of Talheim. Feeling mysteriously empowered by the silent Indian woman whose gaze of unconditional love had x-rayed her soul and set her off on the healing path she was still following today, Annette addressed the group of mourners in a voice torn between an expression of pained tenderness and the need for an adequate volume.

'I'm going to start by reading a poem that I know was close to Eleanor's heart. I introduced her to it, actually, and I know how much it spoke to her. I am sure that many of you will be familiar with it. It's "The Lake Isle of Innisfree" by William Butler Yeats.' She started reading in a loud lilting whisper.

> *I will arise and go now, and go to Innisfree,*
> *And a small cabin build there, of clay and*
> > *wattles made;*
> *Nine bean rows will I have there, a hive for*
> > *the honey bee,*
> *And live alone in the bee-loud glade.*

Whereas it was sophisticated enough to order nine oysters, thought Nicholas, there was something utterly absurd about nine bean rows. Oysters naturally came in dozens and half-dozens – for all he knew, they grew on the seabed in dozens and half-dozens – and so there was something understandably elegant about ordering nine of them. Beans, on the other hand, came in vague fields and profuse heaps, making the prissy precision of nine ridiculous. At the very least it conjured up a dissonant vision of an urban allotment in which there was hardly likely to be room for a clay and wattle cabin and a bee-loud glade. No doubt the Spiritual Tool Box thought that 'Innisfree' was the climax of Yeats's talent, and no doubt the Celtic Twilight, with its wilful innocence and its tawdry effects, was perfectly suited to Eleanor's other-worldly worldview, but in reality the Irish Bard had only emerged from an entirely forgettable mauve mist when he became the mouthpiece for the aristocratic ideal. *'Surely among a rich man's flowering lawns, / Amid the rustle of his planted hills, / Life overflows without ambitious pains; / And rains down life until the basin spills.'* Those were the only lines of Yeats worth memorizing, which was just as well since they were the only ones he could remember. Those lines inaugurated a meditation on the 'bitter and violent' men who performed great deeds and built great houses, and of what happened to that greatness as it turned over time into mere privilege: *'And maybe the great-grandson of that house, / For all its bronze and marble, 's but a mouse.'* A risky line if it weren't for all the great mouse-infested houses one had known. That was why it was so essential, as Yeats was suggesting, to remain bitter and angry, in order to ward off the debilitating effects of inherited glory.

Annette's voice redoubled its excruciated gentleness for the second stanza.

> *And I shall have some peace there, for peace*
> *   comes dropping slow,*
> *Dropping from the veils of the morning to*
> *   where the cricket sings;*
> *There midnight's all a-glimmer, and noon a*
> *   purple glow,*
> *And evening full of the linnet's wings.*

Peace comes dropping slow, thought Henry, how beautiful. The lines lengthening with the growing tranquillity, and the deepening jet lag, and his head dropping slow, dropping slow onto his chest. He needed an espresso, or the veils of morning were going to shroud his mind entirely. He was here for Eleanor, Eleanor on the lake at Fairley, alone in a rowing boat, refusing to come back in, everybody standing on the shore shouting, 'Come back! Your mother's here! Your mother's arrived!' For a girl who was too shy to look you in the eye, she could be as stubborn as a mule.

Where the cricket sings, thought Patrick, is where you live with Seamus in my old home. He imagined the shrill grating coming from the grass and the gradual build-up, cicada by cicada, of pulsing waves of sound, like auditory heat shimmering over the dry land.

Mary was relieved that *plenty o' nuthin'* seemed to have gone down well with Patrick, and she felt that the make-believe simplicity of 'Innisfree' was a charming reminder of Eleanor's yearning to exclude the dark complexities of life at any price. What Mary couldn't relax about was the address she had asked Annette to make. And yet what could she do? There was no point in denying that side of Eleanor's life and Annette was better qualified than anyone else in the room to talk about it. At least it would give Patrick something to rant about for the next few days. She listened to Annette's singsong, cradle-rocking delivery of the final stanza of 'Innisfree' with growing dread.

> *I will arise and go now, for always night and*
>   *day*
> *I hear the lake water lapping with low sounds*
>   *by the shore;*
> *While I stand on the roadway, or on the*
>   *pavements grey,*
> *I hear it in the deep heart's core.*

Annette closed her eyes and reached again for her amber necklace. '*Om namo Matta Meera*,' she murmured, re-empowering herself for the speech she was about to make.

'All of you will have known Eleanor in different ways, and many of you for much longer than me,' she began with an understanding smile. 'I can only talk about the Eleanor that I knew, and while I try to do justice to the wonderful woman that she was, I hope you will hold the Eleanor that you knew in what Yeats calls *the deep heart's core*. But at the same time, if I show you a side of her that you didn't know, all I would ask is that you let her in, let her in and let her join the Eleanor that each of you is holding in your heart.'

Oh, Jesus, thought Patrick, let me out of here. He imagined himself disappearing through the floor with a shovel and some bunk-bed slats, the theme music of *The Great Escape* humming in the air. He was crawling under the crematorium through fragile tunnels, when he felt himself being dragged backwards by Annette's maddening voice.

*

'I first met Eleanor when a group of us from the Dublin Women's Healing Drum Circle were invited down to Saint-Nazaire, her wonderful house in Provence, which I'm sure many of you are familiar with. As we were coming down the drive in our minibus, I caught my first glimpse of Eleanor sitting on the wall of the big pond, with her hands tucked under her thighs, for all the world like a lonely young child staring down at her dangling shoes. By the time we arrived in front of the pond she was literally greeting us with open arms, but I never lost that first impression of her, just as I think she never lost a connection to the child-like quality that made her believe so passionately that justice could be achieved, that consciousness could be transformed and that there was goodness to be found in every person and every situation, however hidden it might seem at first sight.'

Of course consciousness can be transformed, thought Erasmus, but what is it? If I pass an electric current through my body, or bury my nose in the soft petals of a rose, or impersonate Greta Garbo, I transform my consciousness; in fact it is impossible to stop transforming consciousness. What I can't do is describe what it is *in itself*: it's too close to see, too ubiquitous to grasp and too transparent to point to.

'Eleanor was one of the most generous people it has been my privilege to know. You only had to hint that you needed something and if it was in her power to provide it, she would leap at the opportunity with an enthusiasm that made it look as if it was a relief to her rather than to the person who was asking.'

Patrick imagined the simple charm of the dialogue.
 Seamus: I was thinking that it would be, eh, consciousness-raising, like, to own a private hamlet surrounded by vines and olive groves, somewhere sunny.
 Eleanor: Oh, how amazing! I've got one of those. Would you like it?
 Seamus: Oh, thank you very much, I'm sure. Sign here and here and here.
 Eleanor: What a relief. Now I have nothing.

'Nothing,' said Annette, 'was too much trouble for her. Service to others was her life's purpose, and it was awe-inspiring to see the lengths she would go to in her quest to help people achieve their dreams. A torrent of grateful letters and postcards used to arrive at the Foundation from all over the world. A young Croatian scientist who was working on a "zero-energy fuel cell" – don't ask me what that is, but it's going to save the planet – is one example. A Peruvian archaeologist who had uncovered amazing evidence that the Incas were originally from Egypt and continued to communicate with the mother civilization through what he called "solar language". An old lady who had been working for forty years on a universal dictionary of sacred symbols and just needed a little extra help to bring this incredibly valuable book to completion. All of them had received a helping hand from Eleanor. But you mustn't think that Eleanor was only concerned with the higher echelons of science and spirituality, she was also a marvellously practical person who knew the value of a kitchen extension for a growing family, or a new car for a friend living in the depths of the country.'

What about a sister who was running out of cash? thought Nancy grumpily. First they had taken away her credit cards, and then they had taken away her chequebook, and now she had to go in person to the Morgan Guaranty in Fifth Avenue to collect her monthly pocket money. They said it was the only way to stop her running up debts, but the best way to stop her running up debts was to give her more money.

'There was a wonderful Jesuit gentleman,' Annette continued, 'well, he was an ex-Jesuit actually, although we still called him Father Tim. He had come to believe that Catholic dogma was too narrow and that we should embrace all the religious traditions of the world. He eventually became the first Englishman to be accepted as an *ayahuascera* – a Brazilian shaman – among one of the most authentic tribes in Amazonia. Anyhow, Father Tim wrote to Eleanor, who had known him in his old Farm Street days, saying that his village needed a motor-boat to go down to the local trading post, and of course she responded with her usual impulsive generosity, and sent a cheque by return. I shall never forget the expression on her face when she received Father Tim's reply. Inside the envelope were three brightly coloured toucan feathers and an equally colourful note explaining that in recognition of her gift to the Ayoreo people, a ritual had been performed in Father Tim's far-away village inducting her into the tribe as a "Rainbow Warrior". He said that he had refrained from mentioning that she was a woman, since the Ayoreo took a "somewhat unreconstructed view of the gentler sex, not unreminiscent of that taken by old Mother Church", and that he would have "suffered the fate of St. Sebastian" if he "admitted to his ruse". He said that he intended to confess on his deathbed, so as to help move the tribe forward into a new era of harmony between the male and female principles, so necessary to the salvation of the world. Anyhow,' sighed Annette, recognizing that she had drifted from her written text, but taking this to be a sign of inspiration, 'the effect on Eleanor was quite literally magical. She wore the toucan feathers around her neck until they sadly disintegrated, and for a few weeks she told all and sundry that she was an Ayoreo Rainbow Warrior. She was for all the world like the little girl who goes to a new school and comes home one day transformed because she has made a new best friend.'

Although arrested development was his stock in trade and he made a habit of shutting down his psychoanalytic ear when he was not working, Johnny could not help being struck by the ferocious tenacity of Eleanor's resistance to growing up. He was as guilty as anyone of over-quoting good old Eliot's 'Human kind cannot bear very much reality', but he felt that in this case the evasiveness had been uninterrupted. He could remember first meeting Eleanor when Patrick invited him to Saint-Nazaire for the school holidays. Even then she had a habit of lapsing into baby talk, very disconcerting for adolescents distancing themselves from childhood. The tragedy was that five or perhaps ten years of decent five-day-a-week analysis could have mitigated the problem significantly.

'That was the sort of breadth that Eleanor showed in her kindness to others,' said Annette, sensing that it would soon be time to draw her remarks to a conclusion. She put aside a couple of pages she had failed to read during her Amazonian improvisation, and looked down at the last page to remind herself what she had written. It struck her as a little formal now that she had entered into a more exploratory style, but there were one or two things embedded in the last paragraph that she must remember to say.

Oh, please get on with it, thought Patrick. Charles Bronson was having a panic attack in a collapsing tunnel, Alsatians were barking behind the barbed wire, searchlights were weaving over the breached ground, but soon he would be running through the woods, dressed as a German bank clerk and heading for the railway station with some identity papers forged at the expense of Donald Pleasance's eyesight. It would all be over soon, he just had to keep staring at his knees for a few minutes longer.

'I would like to read you a short passage from the *Rig Veda*,' said Annette. 'It quite literally leapt at me from the shelf when I was in the library at the Foundation, looking for a book that would evoke something of Eleanor's amazing spiritual depths.' She resumed her sing-song reading voice.

> *She follows to the goal of those who are passing on beyond, she is the first in the eternal succession of the dawns that are coming, – Usha widens bringing out that which lives, awakening someone who was dead . . . What is her scope when she harmonizes with the dawns that shone out before and those that now must shine? She desires the ancient mornings and fulfils their light; projecting forwards her illumination she enters into communion with the rest that are to come.*

'Eleanor was a firm believer in reincarnation, and not only did she regard suffering as the refining fire that would burn away the impediments to a still higher spiritual evolution, but she was also privileged to have something very rare indeed: a specific vision of how and where she would be reincarnated. At the Foundation we have what we call an "Ah-ha Box" for those little epiphanies and moments of insight when we think, "Ah-ha!" We all have them, don't we? But the trouble is that they slip away during the course of a busy day and so Seamus, the Chief Facilitator of the Foundation, invented the Ah-ha Box so that we could write down our thoughts, pop them in the box and share them in the evening.'

Annette felt the lure of anecdote and digression, resisted for a few seconds, and then caved in. 'We used to have a trainee shaman with a shall I say "challenging" personality, and he was in the habit of having about a dozen Ah-ha moments a day. Many of them turned out to be covert, or not so covert, attacks on other people in the Foundation. Well, one evening when we had all waded through at least ten of his so-called epiphanies, Seamus said, in his incomparably humorous way, "You know, Dennis, one man's Ah-ha moment is another man's Ho-ho moment." And

I remember Eleanor simply cracking up. I can still see her now. She covered her mouth because she thought it would be unkind to laugh too much, but she couldn't help herself. I don't think any portrait of Eleanor would be complete without that naughty giggle and that quick, trusting smile.

'Anyhow,' said Annette, recovering her sense of direction for a final assault, 'as I was saying: one day, after her first stroke but before she moved into the French nursing home, we found this amazing note from Eleanor in the Ah-ha Box. The note said that she had been on a vision quest and she had seen that she would be returning to Saint-Nazaire in her next life-time. She would come back as a young shaman and Seamus and I would be very old by then, and we would hand the Foundation back to her as she had handed it to us in what she called a "seamless conti-nuity". And I would like to end by asking you to hold that phrase, "seamless continuity", in your minds, while we sit here for a few moments in silence and pray for Eleanor's swift return.'

Standing behind the lectern, Annette lowered her head, exhaled solemnly and shut her eyes.

8

Mary thought that 'swift return' was going a bit far. She glanced nervously at the coffin, as if Eleanor might fling off the lid and hop out at any moment, throwing open her arms to embrace the world, with the awkward theatricality of the photograph on the order of service. Sensing Patrick's radiant embarrassment, she regretted asking Annette to make an address, but it was hard to think of anyone who could have spoken instead. Eleanor's slash and burn social life had destroyed continuity and deep friendship, especially after the lonely years of dementia and the fractured relationship with Seamus.

Mary had asked Johnny to read a poem and she had even been desperate enough to get Erasmus to read a passage. Nancy, the only alternative, had been hysterical with self-pity and unclear about when she was getting in from New York. The rather strained choice of readers was balanced (or made worse) by the familiarity of the passages she had chosen. Two great biblical staples were coming up next, and she now felt that it was intolerably boring of her to have picked them. On the other hand, nobody knew anything about death, except that it was unavoidable, and since everyone was terrified by that uncertain certainty, perhaps the opaque magnificence of the Bible, or even the vague Asiatic immensities that Annette obviously preferred, were better than a wilful show of novelty. Besides, Eleanor had been a Christian, amongst so many other things.

As soon as Annette sat down it would be Mary's turn to replace her at the front of the room. The truth was, she was feeling slightly mad. She got up with a reluctance that cunningly disguised itself as a feeling of unbearable urgency, squeezed past Patrick without looking him in the eye and made her way to the lectern. When she told people how nervous she was about any kind of public appearance, they said incredibly annoying things like, 'Don't forget to breathe.' Now she knew why. First she felt that she was going to faint and then, as she started to read the passage she had rehearsed a hundred times, she felt that she was choking as well.

Though I speak with the tongues of men and angels, and have not love, I am become a sounding brass, or a tinkling cymbal. And though I have the gift of prophecy, and understand all mysteries and all knowledge; and though I have all faith, so that I could remove mountains, and have not love, I am nothing. And though I bestow all my goods to feed the poor, and though I give my body to be burned and have not love, it profiteth me nothing.

Mary felt a scratching sensation in her throat, but she tried to persevere without coughing.

Love suffereth long, and is kind; love envieth not: love vaunteth not itself, is not puffed up, doth not behave itself unseemly, seeketh not her own, is not easily provoked, thinketh no evil, rejoiceth not in iniquity, but rejoiceth in the truth; beareth all things, believeth all things, hopeth all things, endureth all things. Love never faileth:

Mary cleared her throat and turned her head aside to cough. Now she had ruined everything. She couldn't help feeling that there was a psychological connection between this part of the passage and her coughing fit. When she had read it yet again this morning, it had struck her as the zenith of false modesty: love boasting about not boasting, love unbelievably pleased with itself for not being puffed up. Until then, it had seemed to be an expression of the highest ideals, but now she was so tired and nervous she couldn't quite shake off the feeling that it was one of the most pompous things ever written. Where was she? She looked at the page with a kind of swimming panic. Then she spotted where she had left off, and pressed forward, feeling that her voice did not quite belong to her.

> but whether there be prophecies, they shall
> fail; whether there be tongues, they shall
> cease; whether there be knowledge, it
> shall vanish away. For we know in part,
> and we prophesy in part. But when that
> which is perfect is come, then that which
> is in part shall be done away.
> When I was a child, I spake as a child,
> I understood as a child: but when I became
> a man, I put away childish things. For now
> we see through a glass, darkly; but then face

to face: now I know in part; but then shall
I know even as also I am known.
And now abideth faith, hope, love, these
three; but the greatest of these is love.

Erasmus had not listened to Mary's reading of St. Paul's Epistle to the Corinthians. Ever since Annette's address, he had been lost in speculation about the doctrine of reincarnation and whether it deserved to be called 'literally nonsensical'. It was a phrase that reminded him of Victor Eisen, the Melrose family's philosopher friend of the sixties and seventies. In philosophical discussions, after a series of vigorous proofs, 'literally nonsensical' used to rush out of him like salt from a cellar that suddenly loses its top. Although he was now a rather faded figure without any enduring work to his name, Eisen had been a fluent and conceited public intellectual during Erasmus's youth. In his eagerness to dismiss, which in the end may have secured his own dismissal, he would certainly have found reincarnation 'literally nonsensical': its evidence-free, memory-free, discarnate narrative failed to satisfy the Parfittian criteria of personal identity. Who is being reincarnated? That was the devastating question, unless the person who was asked happened to be a Buddhist. For him the answer was 'Nobody'. Nobody was reincarnated because nobody had been incarnated in the first place. Something much looser, like a stream of thought, had taken human form. Neither a soul nor a personal identity was needed to precipitate a human life, just a cluster of habits clinging to the hollow concept of independent existence, like a crowd of grasping passengers sinking the lifeboat they imagined would save them. In the background was the ever-present opportunity to slip away into the glittering ocean of a true nature that was not personal either. From this point of view, it was Parfitt and Eisen who were literally nonsensical. Still, Erasmus had no problem with a rejection of reincarnation on the grounds that there was no good reason to believe that it was true – as long as the implicit physicalism of such a rejection was also rejected! The correlation between brain activity and consciousness could be evidence, after all, that the brain was a receiver of consciousness, like a transistor, or a transceiver, and not the skull-bound generator of a private display. The . . .

Erasmus's thoughts were interrupted by the sensation of a hand resting on his shoulder and shaking him gently. His neighbour, after securing his attention, pointed to Mary, who stood in the aisle looking at him significantly. She gave him what he felt was a somewhat curt nod, reminding him that it was his turn to read. He rose with an apologetic smile and, crushing the toes of the woman who had shaken him on the shoulder, made his way towards the front of the room. The passage he had to read was from Revelations – or Obfuscations, as he preferred to call them. Reading it over on the train from Cambridge, he had felt a strange desire to build a time machine so that he could take the author a copy of Kant's *Critique of Pure Reason*.

Erasmus put on his reading glasses, flattened the page against the slope of the lectern, and tried to master his longing to point out the unexamined assumptions that riddled the famous passage he was about to read. He might not be able to infuse his voice with the required feeling of awe and exaltation, but he could at least eliminate any signs of scepticism and indignation. With the inner sigh of a man who doesn't want to be blamed for what's coming next, Erasmus set about his task.

Then I saw a new heaven and a new earth,
for the first heaven and the first earth had
passed away, and the sea was no more.

Nancy was still furious with the clumsy oaf who had stepped on her toes and now, on top of that, he was proposing to take the sea away. No more sea meant no more seaside, no more Cap d'Antibes (although it had been completely ruined), no more Portofino (unbearable in the summer), no more Palm Beach (which was not what it used to be).

And I saw the holy city, new Jerusalem,

Oh, no, not another Jerusalem, thought Nancy. Isn't one enough?

> *coming down out of heaven from God,*
> *prepared as a bride adorned for her*
> *husband; and I heard a great voice from the*
> *throne saying, 'Behold, the dwelling of God*
> *is with men. He will dwell with them and*
> *they shall be his people, and God himself*
> *will be with them; he will wipe away every*
> *tear from their eyes, and death shall be no*
> *more, neither shall there be mourning nor*
> *crying nor pain any more, for the former*
> *things have passed away.'*

All these readings from the Bible were getting on Nancy's nerves. She didn't want to think about death

– it was depressing. At a proper funeral there were amazing choirs that didn't usually sing at private events, and tenors who were practically impossible to get hold of, and readings by famous actors or distinguished public figures. It made the whole thing fun and meant that one hardly ever thought about death, even when the readings were exactly the same, because one was struggling to remember when some tired-looking person had been chancellor of the exchequer, or what the name of their last movie was. That was the miracle of glamour. The more she thought about it, the more furious she felt about Eleanor's dreary funeral. Why, for instance, had she decided to be cremated? Fire was something one dreaded. Fire was something one insured against. The Egyptians had got it right with the pyramids. What could be cosier than something huge and permanent with all one's things tucked away inside (and other people's things as well! Lots and lots of things!) built by thousands of slaves who took the secret of the construction with them to unmarked graves. Nowadays one would have to make prohibitive social-security payments to teams of unionized construction workers. That was modern life for you. Nevertheless, some sort of big monument was infinitely preferable to an urn and a handful of dust.

And he who sat upon the throne said,
'Behold, I make all things new.' Also he
said, 'Write this, for these words are
trustworthy and true.' And he said to me,
'It is done. I am the Alpha and the Omega,
the beginning and the end. To the thirsty
I will give water without price from the
fountain of the water of life. He who
conquers shall have this heritage, and I will
be his God and he will be my son.'

Johnny couldn't help being reminded by all these readings of a paper he had written in his opinionated youth, called 'Omnipotence and Denial: The Lure of Religious Belief.' He had made the simple point that religion inverted everything that we dread about human existence: we're all going to die (we're all going to live for ever); life is terribly unfair (there will be absolute and perfect justice); it's horrible being downtrodden and powerless (the meek shall inherit the earth); and so on. The inversion had to be complete; it was no use saying that life was pretty unfair but not quite as unfair as it sometimes seemed. The pallor of Hades may have been its doom: after making the leap of believing that consciousness did not end with death, a realm of restless shadows pining for blood, muscle, battle and wine must have seemed a thin prize. Achilles said that it was preferable to be a slave on earth than king in the underworld. With that sort of endorsement an afterlife was headed for extinction. Only something perfectly counterfactual could secure global devotion. In his paper Johnny had drawn parallels between this spectacular denial of the depressing and frightening aspects of reality and the operation of the unconscious in the individual patient. He had gone on to make more detailed comparisons between various forms of mental illness and what he imagined to be their corresponding religious discourse, with the disadvantage of knowing nothing about the religious half of the comparison. Feeling that he might as well solve all the world's problems in twelve thousand words, he had tied in political repression with personal repression, and made all the usual points about social control. The underlying assumption of the paper was that authenticity was the only project that mattered and that religious belief necessarily stood in its way. He was now faintly embarrassed by the lack of subtlety and self-doubt in his twenty-nine-year-old self. Still in training, he hadn't yet had a patient, and was therefore much more certain about the operation of the human psyche than he was today.

Mary had asked him to read a long poem by Henry
Vaughan that he had never come across before. She
told him that it fitted perfectly with Eleanor's view
that life was an exile from God, and death a home-
coming. Other, more enjoyable poems had seemed
conventional or irrelevant by contrast, and Mary had
decided to stay loyal to Eleanor's metaphysical nostalgia. As far as Johnny was concerned, giving a religious
status to these moods of longing was just another form
of resistance. Wherever we came from and wherever
we were going (and whether those ideas meant anything at all) it was the bit in between that counted. As
Wittgenstein had said, 'Death is not an event in life:
we do not live to experience death'.

Johnny smiled vaguely at Erasmus as they crossed
paths in the aisle. He balanced his copy of *The Metaphysical Poets* on the ledge of the lectern and opened
it on the page he had marked with a taxi receipt. His
voice was strong and confident as he read.

> *Happy those early days, when I*
> *Shin'd in my Angel-infancy!*
> *Before I understood this place*
> *Appointed for my second race,*
> *Or taught my soul to fancy aught*

But a white celestial thought;
When yet I had not walk'd above
A mile or two from my first Love,
And looking back – at that short space –
Could see a glimpse of His bright face;
When on some gilded cloud or flower
My gazing soul would dwell an hour,
And in those weaker glories spy
Some shadows of eternity;
Before I taught my tongue to wound
My Conscience with a sinful sound,
Or had the black art to dispense
A several sin to ev'ry sense,
But felt through all this fleshly dress
Bright shoots of everlastingness.

Nicholas had started to feel that special sense of claustrophobia he associated with being trapped in chapel at school. Wave after wave of Christian sentiment without even the consolation of an overdue Latin translation tucked furtively in his hymnal. He cheered himself up with his own version of the Christian story: God sent his only begotten son to Earth in order to save the poor, and it was a complete washout, like all half-baked socialist projects; but then the Supreme

Being came to his senses and sent Nicholas to save the rich, and it came to pass that it was an absolute *succès fou*. No doubt with its deplorable history of torture, Inquisition, religious wars, crushing dogma, as well as its altogether more forgivable history of sexual impropriety and worldly self-indulgence, the Roman Catholic Church would look on this crucial development as a heresy; but a heresy was only the prelude to a new Protestant religious order. 'Nicholism' would sweep through what his ghastly American investment adviser called the 'high-net-worth community'. The great question, as always, was what to wear. As the Arch Plutocrat of the Church for the Redemption of Latter-Day Riches one had to cut a dash. Nicholas's imagination wandered back to the page's outfit he had worn as a ten-year-old boy at a very grand royal wedding – the silk breeches, the silver buttons, the buckled shoes . . . he had never felt quite as sure of his own importance since that day.

Johnny renewed his efforts at intonation for the final stanza.

> *O how I long to travel back,*
> *And tread again that ancient track!*
> *That I might once more reach that plain*

Where first I left my glorious train;
From whence th' enlighten'd spirit sees
That shady City of Palm-trees.
But ah! my soul with too much stay
Is drunk, and staggers in the way!
Some men a forward motion love,
But I by backward steps would move;
And when this dust falls to the urn,
In that state I came, return.

Complete rubbish, thought Nicholas, to imply that one returned to the place from which one came. How could it be the same after one's immensely colourful contribution, and how could one's attitude to it be the same after passing through this Vale of Invitations and Sardonic Laughter? He glanced down at the order of service. It looked as if that poem by Vaughan was the last reading. At the bottom of the page there was a note inviting everyone to join the family at the Onslow Club for a drink after the ceremony. He would love to get out of it, but in a moment of reckless generosity he had promised Nancy that he would accompany her. He also had a four o'clock appointment to visit a dying friend at the Chelsea and Westminster Hospital and so it was in fact conveniently nearby. Thank goodness he had booked a car for the day; with distances of that kind (about six hundred yards) one always had to put up with the ill temper of cab drivers who were drifting around the Fulham Road dreaming of a fare to Gatwick or Penzance. He must keep a firm hold on his car; otherwise Nancy would commandeer it for her own purposes. He could easily totter out of the hospital, suffering from the 'compassion burn-out' he knew sometimes afflicted the most heroic nurses, only to find that his car was in Berkeley Square where Nancy was trying to bamboozle a Morgan Guaranty employee into giving her some cash. Her cousin Henry, who had unexpectedly turned up today, had once told him that when he and Nancy were children she had been known as 'the Kleptomaniac'. Little things used to disappear – special hairbrushes, childish jewellery, cherished piggy banks – and turn up in the magpie's nest of Nancy's bedroom. Parents and nannies explained, pedantically at first and then with growing anger, that stealing was wrong, but the temptation was too strong for Nancy and she was expelled from a series of boarding schools for theft and lying. Ever since Nicholas had known her, she had been locked into a state of covetousness, a sense of how much better she would have used, and how much more she deserved, the fabulous possessions belonging to her friends and family. She resisted envying things which belonged to people she didn't know at all, but only to distance herself from her maid, who filled the kitchen with prurient babble about the lives of soap-opera stars. Her recounting of their commonplace 'tragedies' was used to soothe what had been excited by earlier stories of unmerited rewards and ludicrous lifestyles.

Celebrities were all very well for the masses, but what counted for Nicholas was what he called 'the big world', namely the minuscule number of people whose background, looks, or talent to amuse made them worth having to dinner. Nancy belonged to the big world by birth and could not be exiled from that paradise by her perfectly ghastly personality. One had to be loyal to something, and since it offered more scope for treachery than anything except politics, Nicholas was loyal to the big world.

He watched Patrick with a predator's vigilance, hoping for a sign that the ceremony was finally over. Suddenly, the sound system swelled back to life with the brassy opening strains of 'Fly Me to the Moon'.

AT LAST

Fly me to the moon
Let me play among the stars
Let me see what spring is like
On a-Jupiter and Mars

Here we go again, thought Nicholas, off to the bloody moon. Frank Sinatra's voice, oozing with effortless confidence, drove him to distraction. It reminded him of the kind of fun he had not been having in the fifties and sixties. No doubt Eleanor had imagined she was enjoying herself when she lowered the record needle onto a Frank Sinatra single, whizzing round at a giddy forty-five rpm, its discarded sleeve, among the lipstick-smeared glasses of gin and the overflowing ashtrays, displaying a photograph of that sly undistinguished face grinning from the upper reaches of a sky-blue suit.

He continued to stare at Patrick and Mary in the hope that they would leave. Then he saw, to his horror, that it was not Eleanor's son but her coffin that was on the move, sliding forward on steel rollers towards a pair of purple velvet curtains.

In other words, hold my hand
In other words, baby, kiss me

The coffin receded behind the closing curtains and disappeared. Mary got up at last and led the way down the aisle, followed closely by Patrick.

> *Fill my heart with song*
> *And let me sing for ever more*
> *You are all I long for*
> *All I worship and adore*
> *In other words, please be true*
> *In other words, I love you*

Finding himself unexpectedly agitated by the sight of Eleanor's coffin being mechanically swallowed, Nicholas lurched hastily into the aisle, interposing himself between Mary and Patrick. He hobbled forwards, his walking stick reaching eagerly ahead of him, and burst through the doorway into the chill London spring.

9

Patrick stepped into the pallid light, relieved that his mother's funeral was over, but oppressed by the party that still lay ahead. He walked up to Mary and Johnny, who stood under the barely blossoming branches of a cherry tree.

'I don't feel like talking to anyone for a while – except you, of course,' he added politely.

'You don't have to talk to us either,' said Johnny.

'Perfect,' said Patrick.

'Why don't you go ahead with Johnny?' asked Mary.

'Well, if that's all right. Can you . . .'

'Cope with everything,' suggested Mary.

'Exactly.'

They smiled at each other, amused by how typical they were both being.

As Patrick walked to Johnny's car, a plane roared and whistled overhead. He glanced back at the Italianate building he had just left. The campanile encasing the furnace chimney, the low arches of the brick cloister, the dormant rose garden, the weeping willow and the mossy benches formed a masterpiece of decent neutrality.

'I think I'll get cremated here myself,' said Patrick.

'No need to rush,' said Johnny.

'I was going to wait until I died.'

'Good thinking.'

A second plane screeched above them, goading the two men into the muffled interior of the car. Through the railings, beside the Thames, joggers and cyclists bobbed along, determined to stay alive.

'I think my mother's death is the best thing to happen to me since . . . well, since my father's death,' said Patrick.

'It can't be quite that simple,' said Johnny, 'or there would be merry bands of orphans skipping down the street.'

The two men fell silent. Patrick was not in the mood to banter. He felt the presence of a new vitality that could easily be nullified by habit, including the habit of seeming to be clever. Like everyone else, he lived in a world where the same patterns of emotion were projected again and again against the walls of an airless chamber, but just for the moment, he felt the absurdity of mistaking that flickering scene for life. What was the meaning of a feeling he had had forty years ago, let alone one he had refused to have? The crisis was not in the past but in clinging to the past; trapped in a decaying mansion on Sunset Boulevard, forced to watch home movies by a wounded narcissist. Just for the moment he could imagine tiptoeing away from Gloria Swanson, past her terrifying butler, and out into the roar of the contemporary streets; he could imagine the whole system breaking down, without knowing what would happen if it did.

At the little roundabout beyond the crematorium gates, Patrick saw a sign for the Townmead Road Re-Use and Recycling Centre. He couldn't help wondering if Eleanor was being recycled. Poor Eleanor was already muddled enough without being dragged through the dull lights and the dazzling lights and multicoloured mandalas of the Bardo, being challenged by crowds of wrathful deities and hungry ghosts to achieve the transcendence she had run away from while she was alive.

The road ran beside the hedge-filled railings of the

Mortlake Cemetery, past the Hammersmith and Fulham Cemetery, across Chiswick Bridge, and down to the Chiswick Cemetery on the other side. Acre upon acre of gravestones mocking the real-estate ambitions of riverside developers. Why should death, of all nothings, take up so much space? Better to burn in the hollow blue air than claim a plot on that sunless beach, packed side by side in the bony ground, relying on the clutching roots of trees and flowers for a vague resurrection. Perhaps those who had known good mothering were drawn to the earth's absorbing womb, while the abandoned and betrayed longed to be dispersed into the heartless sky. Johnny might have a professional view. Repression was a different kind of burial, preserving trauma in the unconscious, like a statue buried in the desert sand, its sharp features protected from the weather of ordinary experience. Johnny might have views on that as well, but Patrick preferred to remain in silence. What was the unconscious anyway, as against any other form of memory, and why was it given the sovereignty of a definite article, turning it into a thing and a place when the rest of memory was a faculty and a process?

The car climbed the narrow, battered flyover that straddled the Hogarth roundabout. A temporary measure that just wouldn't go away, it had been crying out for replacement ever since Patrick could remember. Perhaps it was the transport equivalent of smoking: never quite the right day to give it up – there's going to be a rush hour tomorrow morning . . . the weekend is coming up . . . let's do this thing after the Olympics . . . 2020 is a lovely round number, a perfect time for a fresh start.

'This dodgy flyover,' said Patrick.

'I know,' said Johnny, 'I always think it's going to collapse.'

He hadn't meant to talk. An inner monologue had broken the surface. Better sink back down, better make a fresh start.

Making a fresh start was a stale start. There was nothing to make and nothing to start, just a continuous breaking out of appearances from potential appearances, like speech from an inner monologue. To be on an equal plane with that articulation: that was freshness. He could feel it in his body, as if in every moment he might cease to be, or continue to be, and that by continuing he was renewed.

'I was just thinking about repression,' said Patrick, 'I don't think that trauma does get repressed, do you?'

'I think that's now the right view,' said Johnny.

'Trauma is too strong and intrusive to be forgotten. It leads to disassociation and splitting off.'

'So, what does get repressed?' asked Patrick.

'Whatever challenges the accommodations of the false self.'

'So there's still plenty of work for it to do.'

'Tons,' said Johnny.

'But there could be no repression at all, no secret burial; just life radiating through us.'

'Theoretically,' said Johnny.

Patrick saw the familiar concrete facade and aquarium-blue windows of Bupa Cromwell Hospital.

'I remember spending a month in there with a slipped disc, just after my father died.'

'And I remember bringing you some extra pain-killers.'

'I salute its ambitious wine list and its action-packed Arabic television channels,' said Patrick, waving majestically at the post-brutalist masterpiece.

The traffic flowed smoothly across the Gloucester Road and down towards the Natural History Museum. Patrick reminded himself to keep quiet. All his life, or at least since he could talk, he had been tempted to flood difficult situations with words. When

Eleanor lost the power to speak and Thomas had not yet acquired it, Patrick discovered a core of inarticulacy in himself that refused to be flooded with words, and which he had tried to flood with alcohol instead. In silence he might see what it was he kept trying to obliterate with talk and drink. What was it that couldn't be said? He could only grope for clues in the darkness of the pre-verbal realm.

His body was a graveyard of buried emotion; its symptoms were clustered around the same fundamental terror, like that rash of cemeteries they had just passed, clustered around the Thames. The nervous bladder, the spastic colon, the lower-back pain, the labile blood pressure that leapt from normal to dangerously high in a few seconds, at the creak of a floorboard or the thought of a thought, and the imperious insomnia that ruled over them all pointed to an anxiety deep enough to disrupt his instincts and take control of the automatic processes of his body. Behaviours could be changed, attitudes modified, mentalities transformed, but it was hard to have a dialogue with the somatic habits of infancy. How could an infant express himself before he had a self to express, or the words to express what he didn't yet have? Only

the dumb language of injury and illness was abun-
dantly available. There was screaming of course, if it
was allowed.

He could remember, when he was three years old,
standing beside the swimming pool in France looking
at the water with apprehensive longing, wishing he
knew how to swim. Suddenly he felt himself being
hoisted off the ground and thrown high in the air.
With the slowness of horror, when the density of
impressions registered by the panic-stricken mind
makes time thicken, he used all the incredulity and
alarm that rushed into his thrashing body to distance
himself from the lethal liquid he had been warned so
often not to fall into by accident, but soon enough he
plunged down into the drowning pool, kicking and
beating the thin water until at last he broke the surface
and sucked in some air before he sank back down
again. He fought for his life in a chaos of jerks and
gulps, sometimes taking in air and sometimes water,
until finally he managed to graze his fingers on the
rough stone edge of the pool and he gave in to sobbing
as quietly as possible, swallowing his despair, knowing
that if he made too much noise his father would do
something really violent and unkind.

David sat in his dark glasses smoking a cigar,

angled away from Patrick, a jaundiced cloud of pastis on the table in front of him, extolling his educational methods to Nicholas Pratt: the stimulation of an instinct to survive; the development of self-sufficiency; an antidote to maternal mollycoddling; in the end, the benefits were so self-evident that only the stupidity and sheepishness of the herd could explain why every three-year-old was not chucked into the deep end of a swimming pool before he knew how to swim.

Robert's curiosity about his grandfather had prompted Patrick to tell him the story of his first swimming lesson. He felt that it would be too burdensome to tell his son about David's beatings and sexual assaults, but at the same time wanted to give Robert a glimpse of his grandfather's harshness. Robert was completely shocked.

'That's so horrible,' he said. 'I mean a three-year-old would think he was dying. In fact, you could have died,' he added, giving Patrick a reassuring hug, as if he sensed that the threat was not completely over.

Robert's empathy overwhelmed Patrick with the reality of what he had taken to be a relatively innocuous anecdote. He could hardly sleep and when he did he was soon woken by his pounding heart. He was hungry all the time but could not digest anything he ate. He could not digest the fact that his father was a man who had wanted to kill him, who would rather have drowned him than taught him to swim, a man who boasted of shooting someone in the head because he had screamed too much, and might shoot Patrick in the head as well, if he made too much noise.

At three of course Patrick would have been able to speak, even if he was forbidden to say what was troubling him. Earlier than that, without the sustenance of narrative, his active memory disintegrated and disappeared. In these darker realms the only clues were lodged in his body, and in one or two stories his mother had told him about his very early life. Here again his father's intolerance of screaming was pivotal, exiling Patrick and his mother to the freezing attic of the Cornish house during the winter he was born.

He sank a little deeper into the passenger seat. As he recognized that he had gone on expecting to be suffocated or dropped, he felt the suffocation and vertigo of the expectations themselves, and if he asked himself whether infancy was destiny, he felt the suffocation and the vertigo of the question. He could feel the weight of his body and the weight on his body. It was like a restraining wall, buckled and sweating from the pressure of the hillside behind it – the only means of access, and at the same time a ferocious guard against the formless miseries of infancy. This was what Johnny might want to call a pre-Oedipal problem, but whatever name was given to a nameless unease, Patrick felt that his tentative new vitality depended on a preparedness to dig into that body of buried emotion and let it join the flow of contemporary feeling. He must pay more attention to the scant evidence that came his way. A strange and upsetting dream had woken him last night, but now it had slipped away and he couldn't get it back.

He understood intuitively that his mother's death was a crisis strong enough to shake his defences. The sudden absence of the woman who had brought him into the world was a fleeting opportunity to bring something slightly new into the world instead. It was important to be realistic: the present was the top layer of the past, not the extravaganza of novelty peddled by people like Seamus and Annette; but even something slightly new could be the layer underneath something slightly newer. He mustn't miss his chance, or his body would keep him living under its misguided heroic strain, like a Japanese soldier who has never been told the news of surrender and continues to booby-trap his patch of jungle and prepare for the honour of a self-inflicted death.

Nauseating as it was to upgrade his father's cruelty to the 'front of the plane' in homicidal class, he felt an even greater reluctance to renounce his childhood view of his mother as the co-victim of David's tempestuous malice. The deeper truth that he had been a toy in the sadomasochistic relationship between his parents was not, until now, something he could bear to contemplate. He clung to the flimsy protection of thinking that his mother was a loving woman who had struggled to satisfy his needs, rather than acknowledging that she had used him as an extension of her lust for humiliation. How self-serving was the story of the freezing attic? It certainly reinforced the picture of Eleanor as a fellow refugee escaping with burns on her back and a baby in her arms from the incendiary bombs of David's rage and self-destruction. Even when Patrick found the courage to tell her that he had been raped by his father, she had rushed to say, 'Me too.' Falling over herself to be a victim, Eleanor seemed indifferent to the impact that her stories might be having at any other level. Suffocated, dropped, born of rape as well as born to be raped – what did it matter, as long as Patrick realized how difficult it had been for her and how far she was from having collaborated with their persecutor. When Patrick asked why she didn't leave, she had said she was afraid that David would kill her, but since he had already twice tried to kill her when they were living together, it was hard to see how living apart would have made it more likely. The truth, which made his blood pressure shoot up as he admitted it, was that she craved the extreme violence of David's presence, and that she threw her son into the bargain. Patrick wanted to stop the car and get out and walk; he wanted a shot of whisky, a shot of heroin, a revolver shot in the head – kill the screaming man, get it over with, be in charge. He let these impulses wash over him without paying them too much attention.

The car was turning into Queensbury Place, next to the Lycée Français de Londres, where Patrick had spent a year of bilingual delinquency when he was seven years old. At the prize-giving ceremony in the Royal Albert Hall, there was a copy of *La Chèvre de Monsieur Seguin* on his red plush seat. He soon became obsessed with the story of the doomed and heroic little goat, lured into the high mountains by the riot of Alpine flowers ('Je me languis, je me languis, je veux aller à la montagne'). Monsieur Seguin, who has already lost six goats to the wolf, is determined not to lose another and locks the hero in the woodshed, but the little goat climbs out through the window and escapes, spending a day of ecstasy on slopes dotted with red and blue and yellow and orange flowers. Then, as the sun begins to set, he suddenly notices among the lengthening shadows the silhouette of the lean and hungry wolf, sitting complacently in the tall grass, contemplating his prey. Knowing he is going to die, the goat nevertheless determines to fight until the dawn ('pourvu que je tienne jusqu'à l'aube'), lowers his head and charges at the wolf's chest. He fights all night, charging again and again, until finally, as the sun rises over the grey crags of the mountain opposite, he collapses on the ground and is destroyed. This story never failed to move Patrick to tears as he read it every night in his bedroom in Victoria Road.

That was it! Last night's strange dream: a hooded figure striding among a herd of goats, pulling their heads back and slitting their throats. Patrick had been one of the goats on the outer edge of the herd and with a sense of doom and defiance worthy of his childhood hero he reached up and tore out his own larynx so as not to give the assassin the satisfaction of hearing him scream. Here was another form of violent silence. If only he had time to work it all out. If only he could be alone, this knot of impressions and connections would untangle at his feet. His psyche was on the move; things that had wanted to be hidden now wanted to be revealed. Wallace Stevens was right: 'Freedom is like a man who kills himself / Each night, an incessant butcher, whose knife / Grows sharp in blood.' He was longing for the splendours of silence and solitude, but instead he was going to a party.

Johnny turned into Onslow Gardens and sped along the suddenly empty stretch of street.

'Here we are,' he said, slowing down to look for a parking space close to the club.

10

Kettle had explained to Mary her principled stand against attending Eleanor's funeral.

'It would be sheer hypocrisy,' she told her daughter. 'I despise disinheritance, and I think it's wrong to go to someone's funeral boiling with rage. The party's a different matter: it's about supporting you and Patrick. I'm not pretending it doesn't help that it's just round the corner.'

'In that case you could look after the boys,' said Mary. 'We feel exactly the same way about their coming to the cremation as you feel about going. Robert disconnected from Eleanor years ago and Thomas never really knew her, but we still want them to come to the party, to mark the occasion for them in a lighter way.'

'Oh, well, of course, I'd be delighted to help,' said

Kettle, immediately determined to get her revenge for being burdened with an even more troublesome responsibility than the one she had been trying to evade.

As soon as Mary had dropped the boys off at her flat, Kettle got to work on Robert.

'Personally,' she said, 'I can't ever forgive your *other* grandmother for giving away your lovely house in France. You must miss it terribly; not being able to go there in the holidays. It was really more of a home than London, I suppose, being in the countryside and all that.'

Robert looked rather more upset than she had intended.

'How can you say that? That's a horrible thing to say,' said Robert.

'I was just trying to be sympathetic,' said Kettle.

Robert walked out of the kitchen and went to sit alone in the drawing room. He hated Kettle for making him think that he should still have Saint-Nazaire. He didn't cry about missing it any more, but he still remembered every detail. They could take away the place but they couldn't take away the images in his mind. Robert closed his eyes and thought about walking back home late one evening with his father through the Butterfly Wood in a high wind. The sound of creaking branches and calling birds was torn away and dissolved among the hissing pines. When they came out of the wood it was nearly night, but he could still make out the gleaming vine shoots snaking through the ploughed earth, and he saw his first shooting star incinerated on the edge of the clear black sky.

Kettle was right: it was more of a home than London. It was his first home and there could only ever be one, but he held it now in his imagination and it was even more beautiful than ever. He didn't want to go back and he didn't want to have it back, because it would be such a disappointment.

Robert had started to cry when Kettle came briskly into the drawing room with Thomas behind her.

'I asked Amparo to get a film for you. If you've got over your tantrum you could watch it with Thomas; she says her grandchildren absolutely love it.'

'Look, Bobby,' said Thomas, running over to show Robert the DVD case, 'it's a flying carpet.'

Robert was furious at the injustice of the word 'tantrum', but he quite wanted to see the film.

'We're not allowed to watch films in the morning,' he said.

'Well,' said Kettle, 'you'll just have to tell your

father you were playing Scrabble, or something fright-fully intellectual that he would approve of.'

'But it's not true,' said Thomas, 'because we're going to see the film.'

'Oh, dear, I can't get anything right, can I?' said Kettle. 'You'll be pleased to hear that silly old Granny is going out for a while. If you can face the treat I've gone to the trouble of organizing, just tell Amparo and she'll put it on for you. If not, there's a copy of the *Telegraph* in the kitchen – I'm sure you can get the crossword puzzle done by the time I'm back.'

With this triumphant sarcasm, Kettle left her flat, a martyr to her spoilt and oversensitive grandsons. She was going to the Patisserie Valerie to have coffee with the widow of our former ambassador to Rome. If the truth be told, Natasha was a frightful bore, always going on about what James would have said, and what James would have thought, as if that mattered any more. Still, it was important to stay in touch with old friends.

Transport by Ford limousine was all part of the Bun-yon's Bronze Service package that Mary had selected for the funeral. Neither the four vintage Rolls-Royces of the Platinum Service, nor the four plumed black

horses and glass-sided carriage of the High Victorian
Service, offered any serious competition. There was
room for three other people in the Ford limo. Nancy
had been Mary's first dutiful choice but Nicholas Pratt
had a car and driver of his own and had already offered
Nancy a lift. In the end, Mary shared the car with Julia,
Patrick's ex-lover; Erasmus, her own ex-lover; and Annette, Seamus's ex-lover. Nobody spoke until the car
was turning, at a mournful pace, onto the main road.

'I hate bereavement,' said Julia, looking at the
mirror in her small powder compact, 'it ruins your
eyeliner.'

'Were you fond of Eleanor?' asked Mary, knowing
that Julia had never bothered with her.

'Oh, it's nothing to do with her,' said Julia, as if
stating the obvious. 'You know the way that tears
spring on you, in a silly film, or at a funeral, or when
you read something in the paper: not really brought
on by the thing that triggers them, but from accumu-
lated grief, I suppose, and life just being so generally
maddening.'

'Of course,' said Mary, 'but sometimes the trigger
and the grief are connected.'

She turned away, trying to distance herself from
the routine frivolity of Julia's line on bereavement. She

glimpsed the pink flowers of a magnolia protesting against the black-and-white half-timbered facade of a mock-Tudor side street. Why was the driver going by Kew Bridge? Was it considered more dignified to take the longer route?

'I didn't put on my eyeliner this morning,' said Erasmus, with the studied facetiousness of an academic.

'You can borrow mine if you like,' said Annette, joining in.

'Thank you for what you said about Eleanor,' said Mary, turning to Annette with a smile.

'I only hope I was able to do justice to a very special lady,' said Annette.

'God yes,' said Julia, reapplying her eyeliner meticulously. 'I do wish this car would stop moving.'

'She was certainly someone who wanted to be good,' said Mary, 'and that's rare enough.'

'Ah, intentionality,' said Erasmus, as if he were pointing out a famous waterfall that had just become visible through the car window.

'Paving the road to Hell,' said Julia, moving on to the other eye with her greasy black pencil.

'Aquinas says that love is "desiring another's good",' Erasmus began.

'Just desiring another is good enough for me,' interrupted Julia. 'Of course one doesn't want them to be run over or gunned down in the street – or not often, anyway. It seems to me that Aquinas is just stating the obvious. Everything is rooted in desire.'

'Except conformity, convention, compulsion, hidden motivation, necessity, confusion, perversion, principle.' Erasmus smiled sadly at the wealth of alternatives.

'But they just create other kinds of desire.'

'If you pack every meaning into a single word, you deprive it of any meaning at all,' said Erasmus.

'Well, even if you think Aquinas is a complete genius for saying that,' said Julia, 'I don't see how "desiring another's good" is the same as desiring others to think you're a goody-goody.'

'Eleanor didn't just want to be good, she was good,' said Annette. 'She wasn't just a dreamer like so many visionaries, she was a builder and a mover and shaker who made a practical difference to lots of lives.'

'She certainly made a practical difference to Patrick's life,' said Julia, snapping her compact closed.

Mary was driven mad by Julia's presumption that she was more loyal than anyone to Patrick's interests. Her fidelity to his infidelity was an act of aggression towards Mary that Julia wouldn't have allowed herself without Erasmus's presence and Patrick's absence. Mary decided to keep a cold silence. They were already in Hammersmith and she was easily furious enough to last until Chelsea.

When Nancy invited Henry to join her in Nicholas's car, he pointed out that he had a car of his own.

'Tell him to follow us,' said Nicholas.

And so Henry's empty car followed Nicholas's full car from the crematorium to the club.

'One knows so many more dead people than living ones,' said Nicholas, relaxing into an abundance of padded black leather while electronically reclining the passenger seat towards Nancy's knees so as to lecture his guests from a more convenient angle, 'although, in terms of sheer numbers, all the people who have ever existed cannot equal the verminous multitude currently clutching at the surface of our once beautiful planet.'

'That's one of the problems with reincarnation: who is being reincarnated if there are more people now than the sum of the people who have ever existed?' said Henry. 'It doesn't make any sense.'

'It only makes sense if lumps of raw humanity are raining down on us for their first round of civilization.

That, I'm afraid, is all too plausible,' said Nicholas, arching his eyebrow at his driver and giving a warning glance to Henry. 'It's your first time here, isn't it, Miguel?'

'Yes, Sir Nicholas,' said Miguel, with the merry laugh of a man who is used to being exotically insulted by his employer several times a day.

'It's no use telling you that you were Queen Cleopatra in a previous lifetime, is it?'

'No, Sir Nicholas,' said Miguel, unable to control his mirth.

'What I don't understand about reincarnation is why we all forget,' complained Nancy. 'Wouldn't it have been more fun, when we first met, to have said, "How are you? I haven't seen you since that perfectly ghastly party Marie-Antoinette gave in the Petit Trianon!" Something like that, something fun. I mean, if it's true, reincarnation is like having Alzheimer's on a huge scale, with each lifetime as our little moment of vivid anxiety. I know that my sister believed in it, but by the time I wanted to ask her about why we forget, she *really* did have Alzheimer's, and so it would have been tactless, if you know what I'm saying.'

'Rebirth is just a sentimental rumour imported from

the vegetable kingdom,' said Nicholas wisely. 'We're all impressed by the resurgence of the spring, but the tree never died.'

'You can get reborn in your own lifetime,' said Henry quietly. 'Die to something and go into a new phase.'

'Spare me the spring,' said Nicholas. 'Ever since I was a little boy, I've been in the high summer of being me, and I intend to go on chasing butterflies through the tall grass until the abrupt and painless end. On the other hand, I do see that some people, like Miguel, for instance, are crying out for a complete overhaul.'

Miguel chuckled and shook his head in disbelief.

'Oh, Miguel, isn't he awful?' said Nancy.

'Yes, madam.'

'You're not supposed to agree with her, you moron,' said Nicholas.

'I thought Eleanor was a Christian,' said Henry, who disliked Nicholas's servant-baiting. 'Where does all this Eastern stuff come from?'

'Oh, she was just generally religious,' said Nancy.

'Most people who are Christian at least have the merit of not being Hindu or Sufi,' said Nicholas, 'just as Sufis have the merit of not being Christian, but religiously speaking, Eleanor was like one of those amazing cocktails that make you wonder what motorway collision could have first combined gin, brandy, tomato juice, crème de menthe, and Cointreau into a single drink.'

'Well, she was always a nice kid,' said Henry stoutly, 'always concerned about other people.'

'That can be a good thing,' admitted Nicholas, 'depending on who the other people are, of course.'

Nancy rolled her eyeballs slightly at her cousin in the back seat. She felt that families should be allowed to say horrible things to one another, but that outsiders should be more careful. Henry looked longingly back at his empty car. Even Nicholas needed to take a rest from himself. As his car sped past Bupa Cromwell Hospital everyone fell silent by mutual consent and Nicholas closed his eyes, gathering his resources for the social ordeal that lay ahead.

After the film, Thomas sat on a cushion and pretended to be riding his own flying carpet. First of all he visited his mother and father, who were at his grandmother's funeral. He had seen photographs of his dead grandmother that made him think he could remember her, but then his mother had told him that he last saw her when he was two and she was living in France and so he realized that he had made up the memory from the photograph. Unless in fact he had a very dim memory of her and the photograph had blown on the tiny little ember of his connection with his granny, like a faint orange glow in a heap of soft grey ash, and for a moment he really could remember when he had sat on his granny's lap and smiled at her and patted her wrinkly old face – his mother said he smiled at her and she was really pleased.

The flying carpet shot on to Baghdad, where Thomas jumped off and kicked the evil sorcerer Jafar over the parapet and into the moat. The princess was so grateful that she gave him a pet leopard, a turban with a ruby in the middle and a lamp with a very powerful and funny genie living in it. The genie was just expanding into the air above him when Thomas heard the front door opening and Kettle greeting Amparo in the hall.

'Have the boys been good?'

'Oh, yes, they love the film, just like my granddaughters.'

'Well, at least I've got that right,' sighed Kettle. 'We must hurry; I have a cab waiting outside. I was so exhausted by my friend's complaining that I had to hail a taxi the moment I got out of the patisserie.'

'Oh, dear, I'm so sorry,' said Amparo.

'It can't be helped,' said Kettle stoically.

Kettle found Thomas cross-legged on a cushion next to the big low table in the middle of the drawing room and Robert stretched on the sofa staring at the ceiling.

'I'm riding on a flying carpet,' said Thomas.

'In that case, you won't need the silly old taxi I've got for us to go to the party.'

'No,' said Thomas serenely, 'I'll find my own way.'

He leant forward and grabbed the front corners of the cushion, tilting sideways to go into a steep left turn.

'Let's get a move on,' said Kettle, clapping her hands together impatiently. 'It's costing me a fortune to keep this taxi waiting. What are you doing staring at the ceiling?' she snapped at Robert.

'Thinking.'

'Don't be ridiculous.'

The two boys followed Kettle into the frail old-fashioned cage of a lift that took them to the ground floor of her building. She seemed to calm down once she told the taxi driver to take them to the Onslow Club, but by then both Robert and Thomas felt too upset to talk. Sensing their reluctance, Kettle started to interrogate them about their schools. After dashing some dull questions against their proud silence, she gave in to the temptation of reminiscing about her own schooldays: Sister Bridget's irresistible charm towards the parents, especially the grander ones, and her high austerity towards the girls; the hilarious report in which Sister Anna had said that it would take 'divine intervention' to make Kettle into a mathematician.

Kettle carried on with her complacent self-deprecation as the taxi rumbled down the Fulham Road. The brothers withdrew into their private thoughts, only emerging when they stopped outside the club.

'Oh, look, there's Daddy,' said Robert, lunging out of the taxi ahead of his grandmother.

'Don't wait for me,' said Kettle archly.

'Okay,' said Thomas, following his brother into the street and running up to his father.

'Hello, Dada,' he said, jumping into Patrick's arms. 'Guess what I've been doing? I've been watching *Aladdin*! Not *bin* Laden but *A*-laddin.' He chuckled mischievously, patting both Patrick's cheeks at once.

Patrick burst out laughing and kissed him on the forehead.

11

As he arrived at the entrance of the Onslow Club, with Thomas still in his arms and Robert walking by his side, Patrick heard the distant but distinct sound of Nicholas Pratt disgorging his opinions on the pavement behind him.

'A celebrity these days is somebody you've never heard of,' Nicholas boomed, 'just as "*j'arrive*" is what a French waiter says as he hurries away from you in a Paris cafe. Margot's fame belongs to a bygone era: one actually knows who she is! Nevertheless, to write five autobiographies is going too far. Life is life and writing is writing and if you write as Margot does, like a glass of water on a rainy day it can only dilute the effect of whatever it was you *used* to do well.'

'You are awful,' said Nancy's admiring voice.

Patrick turned around and saw Nancy, her arm

locked in Nicholas's, with a rather demoralized-looking Henry walking on her other side.

'Who is that funny man?' asked Thomas.

'He's called Nicholas Pratt,' said Patrick.

'He's like Toady in a *very* grumpy mood,' said Thomas.

Patrick and Robert both laughed as much as Nicholas's proximity allowed.

'She said to me,' Nicholas continued in his coy simpering voice, ' "I know it's my fifth book, but there always seems to be more to say." If one says nothing in the first place, there always *is* more to say: there's everything to say. Ah, Patrick,' Nicholas checked himself, 'how thrilling to be introduced, at my advanced age, to a new club.' He peered with exaggerated curiosity at the brass plaque on a white stucco pillar. 'The Onslow Club, I don't remember ever hearing it mentioned.'

He's the last one, thought Patrick, watching Nicholas's performance with cold detachment, the last of my parents' friends left alive, the last of the guests who used to visit Saint-Nazaire when I was a child. George Watford and Victor Eisen and Anne Eisen are dead, even Bridget, who was so much younger than Nicholas, is dead. I wish he would drop dead as well.

Patrick lazily retracted his murderous desire to get rid of Nicholas. Death was the kind of boisterous egomaniac that needed no encouragement. Besides, being free, whatever that might mean, couldn't depend on Nicholas's death, or even on Eleanor's.

Still, her death pointed to a post-parental world that Nicholas's presence was obstructing. His perfectly rehearsed contempt was a frayed cable connecting Patrick to the social atmosphere of his childhood. Patrick's one great ally during his troubled youth had always loathed Nicholas. Victor Eisen's wife, Anne, felt that the nimbus of insanity surrounding David Melrose's corruption had made it seem inevitable, whereas Nicholas's decadence was more like a stylistic choice.

Nicholas straightened up and took in the children.

'Are these your sons?'

'Robert and Thomas,' said Patrick, noticing a strong reluctance to put the increasingly burdensome Thomas down on the pavement next to his father's last living friend.

'What a pity David isn't here to enjoy his grandsons,' said Nicholas. 'He would have ensured at the very least that they didn't spend the whole day in front of the television. He was very worried about the tyranny of the cathode-ray tube. I remember vividly when we had seen some children who were practically giving birth to a television set, he said to me, "I dread to think what all that radiation is doing to their little genitals."'

Patrick was lost for words.

'Let's go inside,' said Henry firmly. He smiled at the two boys and led the party indoors.

'I'm your cousin Henry,' he said to Robert. 'You came to stay with me in Maine a few years back.'

'On that island,' said Robert. 'I remember. I loved it there.'

'You must come again.'

Patrick pressed ahead with Thomas, while Nicholas, like a lame pointer following a wounded bird, hobbled after him across the black-and-white tiles of the entrance hall. He could tell that he had unsettled Patrick and didn't want to lose the chance to consolidate his work.

'I can't help thinking how much your father would have enjoyed this occasion,' panted Nicholas. 'Whatever his drawbacks as a parent, you must admit that he never lost his sense of humour.'

'Easy not to lose what you never had,' said Patrick, too relieved that he could speak again to avoid the mistake of engaging with Nicholas.

'Oh, I disagree,' said Nicholas. 'He saw the funny side of *everything*.'

'He only saw the funny side of things that didn't have one,' said Patrick. 'That's not a sense of humour, just a form of cruelty.'

'Well, cruelty and laughter,' said Nicholas, struggling to take off his overcoat next to the row of brass hooks on the far side of the hall, 'have always been close neighbours.'

'Close without being incestuous,' said Patrick. 'In any case, I have to deal with the people who have come to mourn my mother, however much you may miss my other amazing parent.'

Taking advantage of the tangle that had briefly turned Nicholas's overcoat into a straitjacket, Patrick doubled back to the entrance of the club.

'Ah, look, there's Mummy,' he said, at last releasing Thomas onto the chequerboard floor and following him as he ran towards Mary.

'I hate to sound like Greta Garbo, but "I want to be alone",' said Patrick in a ludicrous Swedish accent.

'Again!' said Mary. 'Why don't these feelings come over you when you *are* alone? That's when you phone up to complain that you don't get invited to parties any more.'

'That's true, but it's not my mother's after-funeral sandwiches that I have in mind. Listen, I'll just whizz around the block, as if I was having a cigarette, and then I promise I'll come back and be totally present.'

'Promises, promises,' said Mary, with an understanding smile.

Patrick saw Julia, Erasmus and Annette coming in behind Mary and felt the stranglehold of social responsibility. He wanted to leave more than ever but at the same time realized that he wouldn't be able to. Annette spotted Nicholas across the hall.

'Poor Nick, he's got into a real muddle with his overcoat,' she said, rushing to his rescue.

'Let me help you with that.' She pulled at Nicholas's sleeve and released his twisted shoulder.

'Thank you,' said Nicholas. 'That fiend, Patrick, saw that I was trussed up like a turkey and simply walked away.'

'Oh, I'm sure he didn't mean to,' said Annette optimistically.

Having parked his car, Johnny arrived and added to the weight of guests forcing Patrick back into the hall. As he was pushed inside by the collective pressure, Patrick saw a half-familiar grey-haired woman stepping into the club with an air of tremendous determination and asking the hall porter if there was a party for Eleanor Melrose's funeral.

He suddenly remembered where he had seen her before. She had been in the Priory at the same time as him. He met her when he was about to leave on his abortive visit to Becky. She had surged up to him at the front door, wearing a dark green sweater and a tweedy skirt, and started to talk in an urgent and over-familiar way, blocking his path to the exit.

'You leaving?' she asked, not pausing for an answer. 'I must say I don't envy you. I love it here. I come here for a month every year, does me the world of good, gets me away from home. The thing is, I absolutely loathe my children. They're monsters. Their father, whose guts I loathe, never disciplined them, so you can imagine the sort of horrors they've turned into. Of course I've had my part to play. I mean, I lay in bed for ten months not uttering a single syllable and then when I did start talking I couldn't stop because of all the things that had piled up during the ten months. I don't know what you're in here for officially, but I have a feeling. No, listen to me. If I have one word of advice it's "Amitriptyline". It's absolutely wonderful. The only time I was happy was when I was on it. I've been trying to get hold of it ever since, but the bastards won't give me any.'

'The thing is I'm trying to stop taking anything,' said Patrick.

'Don't be so stupid; it's the most marvellous drug.'

She followed him out onto the steps after his cab arrived. '*Amitriptyline*,' she shouted, as if he'd been the one to tell her about it, 'you lucky thing!'

He had not followed her fierce advice and taken up Amitriptyline; in fact in the next few months he had given up the oxazepam and the antidepressants and stopped drinking alcohol altogether.

'It's so weird,' said Patrick to Johnny as they climbed the staircase to the room designated for the party, 'a woman arrived just now who was in the Priory at the same time as me last year. She's a complete loony.'

'It's bound to happen in a place like that,' said Johnny.

'I wouldn't know, being completely normal,' said Patrick.

'Perhaps too normal,' said Johnny.

'Just too damn normal,' said Patrick, pounding his fist into his palm.

'Fortunately, we can help you with that,' said

Johnny, in the voice of a wise paternalistic American doctor, 'thanks to Xywyz, a breakthrough medication that only employs the last four letters of the alphabet.'

'That's incredible!' said Patrick, wonder-struck.

Johnny dashed through a rapid disclaimer: 'Do not take Xywyz if you are using water or other hydrating agents. Possible side-effects include blindness, incontinence, aneurism, liver failure, dizziness, skin rash, depression, internal haemorrhaging and sudden death.'

'I don't care,' wailed Patrick, 'I want it anyway. I gotta have it.'

The two men fell silent. They had been improvising little sketches for decades, since the days when they smoked cigarettes and later joints on the fire escape during breaks at school.

'She was asking about this party,' said Patrick, as they reached the landing.

'Maybe she knew your mother.'

'Sometimes the simplest explanations are the best,' Patrick conceded, 'although she might be a funeral fanatic having a manic episode.'

The sound of uncorking bottles reminded Patrick that it was only a year since Gordon, the wise Scottish moderator, had interviewed him before he joined the Depression Group for daily sessions. Gordon drew his attention to 'the alcoholic behind the alcohol'.

'You can take the brandy out of the fruitcake,' he said, 'but you're still left with the fruitcake.'

Patrick, who had spent the night in a state of seething hallucination and cosmic unease, was not in the mood to agree with anything.

'I don't think you can take the brandy out of the fruitcake,' he said, 'or the eggs out of the soufflé, or the salt out of the sea.'

'It was only a metaphor,' said Gordon.

'*Only* a metaphor!' Patrick howled. 'Metaphor is the whole problem, the solvent of nightmares. At the molten heart of things everything resembles everything else: that's the horror.'

Gordon glanced down at Patrick's sheet to make sure he had taken his latest dose of oxazepam.

'What I'm really asking,' he persevered, 'is what have you been self-medicating for, at the end of the day, if not depression?'

'Borderline personality, narcissistic rage, schizoid tendencies . . .' Patrick suggested some plausible additions.

Gordon roared with therapeutic laughter. 'Excellent! You've come in with some self-knowledge under your belt.'

Patrick glanced down the stairwell to make sure the Amitriptyline woman wasn't nearby.

'I saw her twice,' he told Johnny, 'once at the beginning of my stay and once in the middle, when I was starting to get better. The first time she lectured me on the joys of Amitriptyline, but the second time we didn't even talk, I just saw her delivering the same speech to someone from my Depression Group.'

'So, she was a sort of Ancient Mariner of Amitriptyline.'

'Exactly.'

Patrick remembered his second sighting of her very clearly, because it had taken place on the pivotal day of his stay. A raw clarity had started to take over from the withdrawal and delirium of his first fortnight. He spent more and more time alone in the garden, not wanting to drown in the chatter of a group lunch, or spend any more time in his bedroom than he already did. One day he was sitting on the most secluded bench in the garden when he suddenly started to cry. There was nothing in the patch of pasty sky or the partial view of a tree that justified his feeling of aesthetic bliss; no wood pigeons thrummed on the branch, no distant opera music drifted across the lawn, no crocuses shivered at the foot of the tree. Something unseen and unprovoked had invaded his depressive gaze, and spread like a gold rush through the ruins of his tired brain. He had no control over the source of his reprieve. He had not reframed or distanced his depression; it had simply yielded to another way of being. He was crying with gratitude but also with frustration at not being able to secure a supply of this precious new commodity. He felt the depths of his own psychological materialism and saw dimly that it stood in his way, but the habit of grasping at anything that might alleviate his misery was too strong, and the sense of gratuitous beauty that had shimmered through him disappeared as he tried to work out how it could be captured and put to use.

And then the Amitriptyline woman appeared wearing the same green sweater and tweedy skirt that he had first seen her in. He remembered thinking that she must have come with a small suitcase.

'But the bastards won't give me any . . .' she was saying to Jill, a tearful member of Patrick's Depression Group.

Jill had run sobbing out of that morning's session, after her suggestion that the group treat the word 'God' as an acronym for Gift of Desperation had been greeted by the bitter and abrasive Terry with the words, 'Excuse me while I vomit.'

Anxious to avoid conversation with the two women, Patrick bolted behind the dark lateral branches of a cedar tree.

'You lucky thing . . .' The Amitriptyline speech continued on its inevitable course.

'But I haven't been given any,' Jill protested, clearly feeling the presence of God, as tears welled up in her eyes again.

'The last time I saw her, I got stuck behind a cedar tree for twenty minutes,' Patrick explained to Johnny, as they walked into a pale blue room with high French windows overlooking a placid communal garden. 'When I saw her coming, I dashed behind a tree while they took over the bench I'd been sitting on.'

'Serves you right for abandoning your depression buddy,' said Johnny.

'I was having an epiphany.'

'Oh, well . . .'

'It all seems so far away.'

'The epiphany or the Priory?'

'Both,' said Patrick, 'or at least they did until that woman turned up.'

'Maybe insight comes when you need to get out of the madhouse. The loony downstairs might be a catalyst.'

'Anything might be a catalyst,' said Patrick. 'Anything might be evidence, anything might be a clue. We can never afford to relax our vigilance.'

'Fortunately we can help with that,' Johnny slipped again into his American doctor's voice, 'thanks to Vigilante. Fought over by fighter pilots, presiding over presidents, terrifying terrorists, the busy-ness behind the business of America. *Vigilante: "Keeping Our Leaders on the Job Around the Clock."'* Johnny's voice switched to a rapid murmur. 'Do not take Vigilante if you are suffering from high blood pressure, low blood pressure, or normal blood pressure. Consult your physician if you experience chest pains, swollen eyelids, elongated ears . . .'

Patrick tuned out of the disclaimer and looked around at the almost empty room. Nancy was already deep in a plate of sandwiches at the far end of a long table loaded with too much food for the small party of mourners. Henry was standing next to her, talking to Robert. Behind the table was an exceptionally pretty waitress, with a long neck and high cheekbones and short black hair. She gave Patrick a friendly open smile. She must be an aspiring actress between auditions. She was absurdly attractive. He wanted to leave with her straight away. Why did she seem so irresistible? Did the table of almost untouched food make her seem generous as well as lovely? What was the proper approach on such an occasion? My mother just died and I need cheering up? My mother never gave me enough to eat but you look as if you could do much better? Patrick let out a short bark of private laughter at the absurdity of these tyrannical impulses, the depth of his dependency, the fantasy of being saved, the fantasy of being nourished. There was just too much past weighing down on his attention, taking it below the waterline, flooding him with primitive, pre-verbal urges. He imagined himself shaking off his unconscious, like a dog just out of the sea. He walked over to the table, asked for a glass of sparkling water and gave the waitress a simple smile with no future. He thanked her and turned away crisply. There was something hollow about the performance; he still found her utterly adorable, but he saw the attraction for what it was: his own hunger, with no interpersonal implications whatsoever.

He was reminded of Jill from his Depression Group, who had complained one day that she had 'a relationship problem – well, the problem is that the person I have a relationship with doesn't know that we have a relationship'. This confession had elicited peals of derisive laughter from Terry.

'No wonder you're in treatment for the ninth time,' said Terry.

Jill hurried from the room, sobbing.

'You're going to have to apologize for that,' said Gordon.

'But I meant it.'

'That's why you have to apologize.'

'But I wouldn't mean it if I apologized,' Terry argued.

'Fake it to make it, man,' said Gary, the American whose opportunistic tourist of a mother had created such a flurry during Patrick's first Group session.

Patrick wondered if he was faking it to make it – a phrase that had always filled him with disgust – by turning away so resolutely from a woman he would rather have seduced. No, it was the seduction that would have been faking it, the Casanova complex that would have forced him to disguise his infantile yearnings with the appearance of adult behaviour: courtesy, conversation, copulation, commentary – elaborate devices for distancing him from the impotent baby whose screams he could not bear to hear. The glory of his mother's death was that she could no longer get in the way of his own maternal instincts with her presumptive maternal presence and stop him from embracing the inconsolable wreck that she had given birth to.

12

As the room began to fill, Patrick was drawn out of his private thoughts and back into his role as host. Nicholas walked past him with haughty indifference to join Nancy at the far end of the room. Mary came over with the Amitriptyline woman in tow, followed closely by Thomas and Erasmus.

'Patrick,' said Mary, 'you should meet Fleur, she's an old friend of your mother's.'

Patrick shook hands with her politely, marvelling at her whimsical French name. Now that she had taken off her overcoat he could see the green sweater and tweed skirt he recognized from the Priory. Bright red lipstick in the shape of a mouth shadowed Fleur's own mouth, about half an inch to the right, giving the impression of a circus clown caught in the middle of removing her make-up.

'How did you know . . .' Patrick began.

'Dada!' said Thomas, too excited not to interrupt. 'Erasmus is a real philosopher!'

'Or at any rate a realist philosopher,' said Erasmus.

'I know, darling,' said Patrick, ruffling his son's hair. Thomas hadn't seen Erasmus for a year and a half, and clearly the category of philosopher had come into focus during that time.

'I mean,' said Thomas, looking very philosophical, 'I always think the trouble with God is: Who created God? And,' he added, getting into the swing of it, 'who created whoever created God?'

'Ah, an infinite regress,' said Erasmus sadly.

'Okay, then,' said Thomas, 'who created infinite regress?' He looked up at his father to check that he was arguing philosophically.

Patrick gave him an encouraging smile.

'He's frightfully clever, isn't he?' said Fleur. 'Unlike my lot: they could hardly string a sentence together until they were well into their teens, and then it was only to insult me – and their father, who deserved it of course. Absolute monsters.'

Mary slipped away with Thomas and Erasmus, leaving Patrick stranded with Fleur.

'That's teenagers for you,' said Patrick, with resolute blandness. 'So, how did you know Eleanor?'

'I adored your mother. I think she was one of the very few good people I ever met. She saved my life really – I suppose it must have been thirty years ago – by giving me a job in one of the charity shops she used to run for the Save the Children Fund.'

'I remember those shops,' said Patrick, noticing that Fleur was gathering momentum and didn't want to be interrupted.

'I was thought by some people,' Fleur motored on, 'well, by everyone except your mother really, to be unemployable, because of my episodes, but I simply had to get out of the house and *do* something, so your mother was an absolute godsend. She had me packing up second-hand clothes in no time. We used to send them off to the shop we thought they'd do best in, keeping the really good ones for our shop in Launceston Place, just round the corner from your house.'

'Yes,' said Patrick quickly.

'We used to have such fun,' Fleur reminisced, 'we were like a couple of schoolgirls, holding up the clothes and saying, "Richmond, I think," or "*Very* Cheltenham." Sometimes we'd both shout, "Rochdale!" or,

"Hemel Hempstead!" at exactly the same time. Oh, how we laughed. Eventually your mother trusted me enough to put me on the till and let me run the shop for the whole day, and that, I'm afraid, is when I had one of my episodes. We had a fur coat in that morning – it was the time when people started to get paint thrown at them if they wore one – an amazing sable coat – I think that's what tipped me over the edge. I was gripped by a need to do something really glamorous, so I shut up the shop and took all the money from the till and put on the sable coat – it wasn't very suitable at the height of June, but I had to wear it. Anyway, I went out and hailed a cab and said, "Take me to the Ritz!" '

Patrick looked around the room anxiously, wondering if he would ever get away.

'They tried to take my coat off me,' Fleur accelerated, 'but I wouldn't hear of it, and so I sat in the Palm Court in a heap of sable, drinking champagne cocktails and talking to anyone who would listen, until a frightfully pompous head waiter asked me to leave because I was being "a nuisance to the other guests"! Can you imagine the rudeness of it? Well, anyway, the money I'd taken from the till turned out not to be enough for the enormous bill and so the wretched hotel insisted on

keeping the coat, which turned out to be very inconvenient because the lady who had given it to us came
back and said she'd changed her mind . . .'

By now Fleur was falling over herself to keep up
with her thoughts. Patrick tried to catch Mary's eye,
but she seemed to be deliberately ignoring him.

'All I can say is that your mother was absolutely
marvellous. She went and paid the bill and rescued the
coat. She said she was used to it because she was
always clearing her father's bar bills in grand places,
and she didn't mind at all. She was an absolute saint
and let me go on running the shop when she was
away, saying that she was sure I wouldn't do it again
– which I'm afraid to say I did, more than once.'

'Would you like a drink?' asked Patrick, turning
back towards the waitress with renewed longing. Perhaps he should run away with her after all. He wanted
to kiss the pulse in her long neck.

'I shouldn't really but I'll have a gin and tonic,' said
Fleur, hardly pausing before she continued. 'You must
be very proud of your mother. She did an enormous
amount of practical good, the only sort of good there
is really – touched on hundreds of lives, threw herself
into those shops with tremendous energy – I firmly
believe she could have been an entrepreneur, if she had

needed the money – the way she used to set off to the Harrogate Trade Fair with a spring in her step.'

Patrick smiled at the waitress and then looked down at the tablecloth bashfully. When he looked up again she was smiling at him with sympathy and laughter in her eyes. She clearly understood everything. She was wonderfully intelligent as well as impossibly lovely. The more Fleur talked about Eleanor, the more he wanted to start a new life with the waitress. He took the gin and tonic from her tenderly and handed it on to the loquacious Fleur, who seemed to be saying, 'Well, do you?' for reasons he couldn't fathom.

'Do I what?' he asked.

'Feel proud of your mother?'

'I suppose so,' said Patrick.

'What do you mean, you "suppose so"? You're worse than my children. Absolute monsters.'

'Listen, it's been a great pleasure to meet you,' said Patrick, 'and I expect we'll talk again, but I probably ought to circulate.'

He moved away from Fleur unceremoniously and, wanting to look as if he had a firm intention, walked towards Julia, who stood alone by the window drinking a glass of white wine.

'Help!' said Patrick.

'Oh, hi,' said Julia, 'I was just staring out of the window vacantly, but not so vacantly that I didn't see you flirting with that pretty waitress.'

'Flirting? I didn't say a word.'

'You didn't have to, darling. A dog doesn't have to say a word when it sits next to us in the dining room making little whimpering sounds while strings of saliva dangle down to the carpet; we still know what it wants.'

'I admit that I was vaguely attracted to her, but it was only after that grey-haired lunatic started talking to me that she began to look like the last overhanging tree before the roar of the rapids.'

'How poetic. You're still trying to be saved.'

'Not at all; I'm trying not to want to be saved.'

'Progress.'

'Relentless forward motion,' said Patrick.

'So who is this lunatic who forced you to flirt with the waitress?'

'Oh, she used to work in my mother's charity shop years ago. Her experience of Eleanor was so different from mine, it made me realize that I'm not in charge of the meaning of my mother's life, and that I'm deluded to think that I can come to some magisterial conclusion about it.'

'Surely you could come to some conclusion about what it means to you.'

'I'm not even sure if that's true,' said Patrick. 'I've been noticing today how inconclusive I feel about both my parents. There isn't any final truth; it's more like being able to get off on different floors of the same building.'

'It sounds awfully tiring,' Julia complained. 'Wouldn't it be simpler to just loathe their guts?'

Patrick burst out laughing.

'I used to think that I was detached about my father. I thought that detachment was the great virtue, without the moral condescension built into forgiveness, but the truth is that I feel everything: contempt, rage, pity, terror, tenderness and detachment.'

'Tenderness?'

'At the thought of how unhappy he was. When I had sons of my own and felt the strength of my instinct to protect them, I was freshly shocked that he had deliberately inflicted harm on his son, and then the hatred returned.'

'So you've pretty much abandoned detachment.'

'On the contrary, I just recognize how many things there are to be detached about. The incandescent hatred and the pure terror don't invalidate the detachment, they give it a chance to expand.'

'The StairMasters of detachment,' said Julia.

'Exactly.'

'I wonder if I'm allowed to smoke out here,' said Julia, opening the French windows and stepping outside. Patrick followed her onto the narrow balcony and sat on the edge of the white stucco balustrade. As she took out her packet of Camel Blue, his eyes traced the elegant profile he had often studied from a neighbouring pillow, now set against the restrained promise of the still-leafless trees. He watched Julia kiss the filter of her cigarette and suck the swaying flame of her lighter into the tightly packed tobacco. After the first immense drag, smoke flowed over her upper lip, only to be drawn back through her nose into her expanding lungs and eventually released, at first in a single thick stream and then in the little puffs and misshapen rings and drifting walls formed by her smoky words.

'So, have you been working out especially hard on your Inner StairMaster today?'

'I've felt a strange mixture of elation and free-fall. There's something cool and objective about death compared to the savage privacy of dying which my mother's illness forced me to imagine over the last four years. In a sense I can think about her clearly for the first time, away from the vortex of an empathy that was neither compassionate nor salutary, but a kind of understudy to her own horror.'

'Wouldn't it be even better not to think about her at all?' said Julia with a second languorous gulp of cigarette smoke.

'No, not today,' said Patrick, suddenly repelled by Julia's enamelled surface.

'Oh, of course, not today – of all days,' said Julia, sensing his defection. 'I just meant eventually.'

'The people who tell us to "get over it" and "get on with it" are the least able to have the direct experience that they berate navel-gazers for avoiding,' said Patrick, in the prosecuting style he adopted when defending himself. 'The "it" they're "getting on with" is a ghostly re-enactment of unreflecting habits. Not thinking about something is the surest way to remain under its influence.'

'It's a fair cop, guv,' said Julia, disconcerted by Patrick's sincerity.

'What would it mean to be spontaneous, to have an unconditioned response to things – to anything?

Neither of us is in a position to know, but I don't want to die without finding out.'

'Hmm,' said Julia, clearly not tempted by Patrick's obscure project.

'Excuse me,' said a voice behind them.

Patrick looked round and saw the beautiful waitress. He had forgotten that he was in love with her, but now it all came back to him.

'Oh, hi,' he said.

She scarcely acknowledged him, but kept her eyes fixed on Julia.

'I'm sorry but you're not allowed to smoke out here,' she said.

'Oh, dear,' said Julia, taking a drag on her cigarette, 'I didn't know. It's funny, because it is outside.'

'Well, technically it's still part of the club and you can't smoke anywhere in the club.'

'I understand,' said Julia, continuing to smoke. 'Well, I'd better put it out then.' She took another long suck on her almost finished cigarette, dropped it on the balcony and ground it underfoot before stepping back indoors.

Patrick waited for the waitress to look at him with complicity and amusement, but she returned to her post behind the long table without glancing in his direction.

The waitress was useless. Julia was useless. Eleanor was useless. Even Mary in the end was useless and would not prevent him from returning to his bedsit alone and without any consolation whatever.

It was not the women who were at fault; it was his omnipotent delusion: the idea that they were there to be useful to him in the first place. He must make sure to remember that the next time one of the pointless bitches let him down. Patrick let out another bark of laughter. He was feeling a little bit mad. Casanova, the misogynist; Casanova, the hungry baby. The inadequacy at the rotten heart of exaggeration. He watched a modest veil of self-disgust settle on the subject of his relations with women, trying to prevent him from going deeper. Self-disgust was the easy way out, he must cut through it and allow himself to be unconsoled. He looked forward to the austere demands of that word, like a cool drink after the dry oasis of consolation. Back in his bedsit unconsoled, he could hardly wait.

It was getting cold on the balcony and Patrick wanted to get back indoors, but he was prevented by his reluctance to join Kettle and Mary, who were standing just the other side of the French windows.

'I see that you and Thomas are still practically glued to each other,' said Kettle, casting an envious glance at her grandson draped comfortably around his mother's neck.

'Nobody can hope to ignore their children as completely as you did,' sighed Mary.

'What do you mean? We always . . . communicated.'

'Communicated! Do you remember what you said to me when you telephoned me at school to tell me that Daddy had died?'

'How awful it all was, I suppose.'

'I couldn't speak I was so upset, and you told me to *cheer up*. To *cheer up*! You never had any idea who I was and you still don't.'

Mary turned away with a growl of exasperation and walked towards the other end of the room. Kettle greeted the inevitable outcome of her spite with an expression of astonished incomprehension. Patrick hovered on the balcony waiting for her to move away, but watched instead as Annette came up to engage her in conversation.

'Hello, dear,' said Annette, 'how are you?'

'Well, I've just had my head bitten off by my daughter, and so just for the moment I'm in a state of shock.'

'Mothers and children,' said Annette wisely, 'maybe we should have a workshop on that dynamic and tempt you back to the Foundation.'

'A workshop on mothers and children would tempt me to stay away,' said Kettle. 'Not that I need much encouragement to stay away; I think I've finished with shamanism.'

'Bless you,' said Annette. 'I won't feel that I've finished until I'm totally connected to the source of unconditional love that inhabits every soul on this planet.'

'Well, I've set my sights rather lower,' said Kettle. 'I think I'm just relieved not to be shaking a rattle, with my eyes watering from all that wretched wood smoke.'

Annette let out a peal of tolerant laughter.

'Well, I know Seamus would love to see you again and that he thought you'd especially benefit from our "Walking with the Goddess" workshop, "stepping into the power of the feminine". I'm going to be participating myself.'

'How is Seamus? I suppose he's moved into the main house now.'

'Oh, yes, he's in Eleanor's old bedroom, lording it over all of us.'

'The bedroom Patrick and Mary used to be in, with the view of the olive groves?'

'Oh, that's a glorious view, isn't it? Mind you, I love my room, looking out on the chapel.'

'That's my room,' said Kettle. 'I always used to stay in that room.'

'Isn't it funny how we get attached to things?' laughed Annette. 'And yet, in the end, even our bodies aren't really our own; they belong to the Earth – to the Goddess.'

'Not yet,' said Kettle firmly.

'I tell you what,' said Annette, 'if you come to the Goddess workshop, you can have your old room back. I don't mind moving out; I'm happy anywhere. Anyway, Seamus is always talking about "moving from the property paradigm to the participation paradigm", and if the facilitators at the Foundation don't do it, we can't expect anyone else to.'

Patrick's primary objective was to get off the balcony without drawing attention to himself, and so he suppressed the desire to point out that Seamus had been moving in the opposite direction, from participating in Eleanor's charity to occupying her property.

Kettle was clearly confused by Annette's kind offer of her old bedroom. Her loyalty to her bad mood was not easily shaken and yet it was hard to see what she could do except thank Annette.

'That's unusually kind of you,' she said dismissively.

Patrick seized his chance and bolted off the balcony, passing behind Kettle's back with such decisiveness that he knocked her into Annette's clattering cup of tea.

'Mind out,' snapped Kettle before she could see who had barged into her. 'Honestly, Patrick,' she added when she saw the culprit.

'Oh, dear, you're covered in tea,' said Annette.

Patrick did not pause and only called 'Sorry' over his shoulder as he crossed the room at a quick pace. He continued out onto the landing and, without knowing where he was going, cantered down the staircase with a light hand on the banister, like a man who had been called away on urgent business.

13

Mary smiled at Henry from across the room and started to move in his direction, but before she could reach his side Fleur surged up in front of her.

'I hope I haven't offended your husband,' she said. 'He walked away from me very abruptly and now he seems to have stormed out of the room altogether.'

'It's a difficult day for him,' said Mary, fascinated by Fleur's lipstick, which had been reapplied, mostly to the old lopsided track around her mouth but also to her front teeth.

'Has he had mental-health problems?' said Fleur. 'I only ask because – God knows! – I've had my fair share and I've grown rather good at telling when other people have a screw loose.'

'You seem quite well now,' said Mary, lying virtuously.

'It's funny you should say that,' said Fleur, 'because this morning I thought, "There's no point in taking your pills when you feel so well." I feel very, very well, you see.'

Mary recoiled instinctively. 'Oh, good,' she said.

'I feel as if something amazing is going to happen to me today,' Fleur went on. 'I don't think I've ever achieved my full potential – I feel as if I could do anything – as if I could raise the dead!'

'That's the last thing anyone would expect at this party,' said Mary, with a cheerful laugh. 'Do ask Patrick first if it's Eleanor you've got in mind.'

'Oh, I'd love to see Eleanor again,' said Fleur, as if endorsing Mary's candidate for resurrection and about to perform the necessary operation.

'Will you excuse me?' said Mary. 'I've got to go and talk to Patrick's cousin. He's come all the way from America and we didn't even know he was coming.'

'I'd love to go to America,' said Fleur, 'in fact, I might fly there later this afternoon.'

'In a plane?' said Mary.

'Yes, of course ... Oh!' Fleur interrupted herself. 'I see what you mean.'

She stuck out her arms, thrust her head forwards

and swayed from side to side, with an explosion of laughter so loud that Mary could sense everyone in the room looking in her direction.

She reached out and touched Fleur's outstretched arm, smiling at her to show how much she had enjoyed sharing their delightful joke, but turning away firmly to join Henry, who stood alone in the corner of the room.

'That woman's laugh packs quite a punch,' said Henry.

'Everything about her packs a punch, that's what I'm worried about,' said Mary. 'I feel she may do something very crazy before we all get home.'

'Who is she? She's kind of exotic.'

Mary noticed how distinct Henry's eyelashes were against the pale translucence of his eyes.

'None of us has ever met her. She just turned up unexpectedly.'

'Like me,' said Henry, with egalitarian gallantry.

'Except that we know who you are and we're very pleased to see you,' said Mary, 'especially since not a lot of people have turned up. Eleanor lost touch with people; her social life was very disintegrated. She had a few little pockets of friendship, each assuming that there was something more central, but in fact there was nothing in the middle. For the last two years, I was the only person who visited her.'

'And Patrick?'

'No, he didn't go. She became so unhappy when she saw him. There was something she was dying to say but couldn't. I don't just mean in the mechanical sense that she couldn't speak in the last two years. I mean that she never could have said what she wanted to tell him, even if she had been the most articulate person in the world, because she didn't know what it was, but when she became ill she could feel the pressure of it.'

'Just horrible,' said Henry. 'It's what we all dread.'

'That's why we must drop our defences while it's still a voluntary act,' said Mary, 'otherwise they'll be demolished and we'll be flooded with nameless horror.'

'Poor Eleanor, I feel so sorry for her,' said Henry.

They both fell silent for a while.

'At this point the English usually say, "Well, this is a cheerful subject!" to cover their embarrassment at being serious,' said Mary.

'Let's just stick with the sorrow,' said Henry with a kind smile.

'I'm really pleased you came,' she said. 'Your love

for Eleanor was so uncomplicated, unlike everyone else's.'

'Cabbage,' said Nancy, grabbing Henry's arm, with the exaggerated eagerness of a shipwrecked passenger who discovers that she is not the only member of her family left alive, 'thank God! Save me from that dreadful woman in the green sweater! I can't believe my sister ever knew her – socially. I mean, this really is the most extraordinary gathering. I don't feel it's really a Jonson occasion at all. When I think of Mummy's funeral, or Aunt Edith's. Eight hundred people turned up at Mummy's, half the French cabinet, and the Aga Khan, and the Windsors; *everybody* was there.'

'Eleanor chose a different path,' said Henry.

'More like a goat track,' said Nancy, rolling her eyes.

'Personally, I don't give a damn who comes to my funeral,' said Henry.

'That's only because you know that it'll be solid with senators and glamorous people and sobbing women!' said Nancy. 'The trouble with funerals is that they're so last-minute. That's where memorials come in, of course, but they're not the same. There's something so dramatic about a funeral, although I can't abide those open caskets. Do you remember Uncle Vlad? I still have nightmares about him lying there in that gold and white uniform looking all *gaunt*. Oh, God, wagon formation,' cried Nancy, 'the green goblin is staring at me again!'

Fleur was feeling a sense of irrepressible pleasure and potency as she scanned the room for someone who had not yet had the benefit of her conversation. She could understand all the currents flowing through the room; she only had to glance at a person to see into the depths of their soul. Thanks to Patrick Melrose, who was distracting the waitress by getting her telephone number, Fleur had been able to mix her own drink, a glass full of gin with a splash of tonic, rather than the other way round. What did it matter? Mere alcohol could not degrade her luminous awareness. After taking a gulp from her lipstick-smudged tumbler, she walked up to Nicholas Pratt, determined to help him understand himself.

'Have you had mental-health problems?' she asked Nicholas, fixing him with an intrepid stare.

'Have we met?' said Nicholas, gazing icily at the stranger who stood in his path.

'I only ask because I have a feeling for these things,' Fleur went on.

Nicholas hesitated between the impulse to utterly destroy this batty old woman in a moth-eaten sweater, and the temptation to boast about his robust mental health.

'Well, have you?' insisted Fleur.

Nicholas raised his walking stick briefly, as if about to nudge Fleur aside, only to replant it more firmly in the carpet and lean into its full support. He inhaled the frosty, invigorating air of contempt flooding in from the window smashed by Fleur's impertinent question; contempt that always made him, though he said it himself, even more articulate than usual.

'No, I have not had "mental-health problems",' he thundered. 'Even in this degenerate age of confession and complaint we have not managed to turn reality entirely on its head. When the vocabulary of Freudian mumbo-jumbo is emptied onto every conversation, like vinegar onto a newspaper full of sodden chips, some of us choose not to *tuck in*.' Nicholas craned his head forward as he spat out the homely phrase.

'The sophisticated cherish their "syndromes",' he continued, 'and even the most simple-minded fool feels entitled to a "complex". As if it weren't ludicrous enough for every child to be "gifted", they now have to be ill as well: a touch of Asperger's, a little autism;

dyslexia stalks the playground; the poor little gifted things have been "bullied" at school; if they can't confess to being abused, they must confess to being abusive. Well, my dear woman,' Nicholas laughed threateningly, ' – I call you "my dear" from what is no doubt known as *Sincerity Deficit Disorder*, unless some ambitious quack, landing on the scalding, sarcastic beaches of the great continent of irony, has claimed the inversion of surface meaning as *Potter's Disease* or *Jones's Jaundice* – no, my *dear* woman, I have not suffered from the slightest taint of mental illness. The modern passion for pathology is a landslide that has been forced to come to a halt at some distance from my eminently sane feet. I have only to walk towards that heap of refuse for it to part, making way for the impossible man, the man who is entirely well; psychotherapists scatter in my presence, ashamed of their sham profession!'

'You're completely off your rocker,' said Fleur, discerningly. 'I thought as much. I've developed what I call "my little radar" over the years. Put me in a room full of people and I can tell straight away who has had *that* sort of problem.'

Nicholas experienced a moment of despair as he

realized that his withering eloquence had made no impact, but like an expert tango dancer who turns abruptly on the very edge of the dance floor, he changed his approach and shouted, 'Bugger off!' at the top of his voice.

Fleur looked at him with deepening insight.

'A month in the Priory would get you back on your feet,' she concluded, 're-clothe you in your rightful mind, as the hymn says. Do you know it?' Fleur closed her eyes and started to sing rapturously, ' "Dear Lord and Father of mankind / Forgive our foolish ways / Re-clothe us in our rightful minds . . ." Marvellous stuff. I'll have a word with Dr. Pagazzi, he's quite the best. He can be rather severe at times, but only for one's own good. Look at me: I was mad as a hatter and now I'm on top of the world.'

She leant forward to whisper confidentially to Nicholas.

'I feel very, very well, you see.'

There were professional reasons for Johnny not to engage with Nicholas Pratt, whose daughter had been a patient of his, but the sight of that monstrous man bellowing at a dishevelled old woman pushed his restraint beyond the limits he had imposed on himself until now. He approached Fleur and, with his back turned to Nicholas, asked her quietly if she was all right.

'All right?' laughed Fleur. 'I'm extremely well, better than ever.' She struggled to express her sense of abundance. 'If there were such a thing as being too well, I'd be it. I was just trying to help this poor man who's had more than his fair share of mental-health problems.'

Reassured that she was unharmed, Johnny smiled at Fleur and started to withdraw tactfully, but Nicholas was by now too enraged to let such an opportunity pass.

'Ah,' he said, 'here he is! Like an exhibit in a courtroom drama, brought on at the perfect moment: a practising witch-doctor, a purveyor of psycho-*paralysis*, a guide to the catacombs, a guide to the sewers; he promises to turn your dreams into nightmares and he keeps his promises religiously,' snarled Nicholas, his face flushed and the corners of his mouth flecked with tired saliva. 'The ferryman of Hell's second river won't accept a simple coin, like his proletarian colleague on the Styx. You'll need a fat cheque to cross the Lethe into that forgotten underworld of dangerous gibberish where toothless infants rip the nipples from their mothers' milkless breasts.'

Nicholas seemed to be labouring for breath, as he unrolled his vituperative sentences.

'No fantasy that you invent,' he struggled on, 'could be as repulsive as the fantasy on which his sinister art is based, polluting the human imagination with murderous babies and incestuous children . . .'

Nicholas suddenly stopped speaking, his mouth working to take in enough air. He rocked sideways on his walking stick before staggering backwards a couple of steps and crashing down against the table and onto the floor. He caught the tablecloth as he fell and dragged half a dozen glasses after him. A bottle of red wine toppled sideways and its contents gurgled over the edge of the table and splashed onto his black suit. The waitress lunged forward and caught the bucket of half-melted ice that was sliding towards Nicholas's supine body.

'Oh, dear,' said Fleur, 'he got himself too worked up. "Hoisted by his own petard", as the saying goes. This is what happens to people who won't ask for help,' she said, as if discussing the case with Dr. Pagazzi.

Mary leant over to the waitress, her mobile phone already open.

'I'm going to call an ambulance,' she said.

'Thanks,' said the waitress. 'I'll go downstairs and warn reception.'

Everyone in the room gathered around the fallen figure and looked on with a mixture of curiosity and alarm.

Patrick knelt down beside Nicholas and started to loosen his tie. Long after it could have been helpful, he continued to loosen the knot until he had removed the tie altogether. Only then did he undo the top button of Nicholas's shirt. Nicholas tried to say something but winced from the effort and closed his eyes instead, disgusted by his own vulnerability.

Johnny acknowledged a feeling of satisfaction at having played no active part in Nicholas's collapse. And then he looked down at his fallen opponent, sprawled heavily on the carpet, and somehow the sight of his old neck, no longer festooned with an expensive black silk tie, but wrinkled and sagging and open at the throat, as if waiting for the final dagger thrust, filled him with pity and renewed his respect for the conservative powers of an ego that would rather kill its owner than allow him to change.

'Johnny?' said Robert.

'Yes,' said Johnny, seeing Robert and Thomas looking up at him with great interest.

'Why was that man so angry with you?'

'It's a long story,' said Johnny, 'and one that I'm not really allowed to tell.'

'Has he got psycho-paralysis?' said Thomas. 'Because paralysis means you can't move.'

Johnny couldn't help laughing, despite the solemn murmur surrounding Nicholas's collapse.

'Well, personally, I think that would be a brilliant diagnosis; but Nicholas Pratt invented that word in order to make fun of psychoanalysis, which is what I do for a job.'

'What's that?' said Thomas.

'It's a way of getting access to hidden truths about your feelings,' said Johnny.

'Like hide and seek?' said Thomas.

'Exactly,' said Johnny, 'but instead of hiding in cupboards and behind curtains and under beds, this kind of truth hides in symptoms and dreams and habits.'

'Can we play?' said Thomas.

'Can we stop playing?' said Johnny, more to himself than to Thomas and Robert.

Julia came up and interrupted Johnny's conversation with the children.

'Is this the end?' she said. 'It's enough to put one off having a temper tantrum. Oh, God, that religious fanatic is cradling his head. That would definitely finish me off.'

Annette was sitting on her heels next to Nicholas, with her hands cupped around his head, her eyes closed and her lips moving very slightly.

'Is she praying?' said Julia, flabbergasted.

'That's nice of her,' said Thomas.

'They say one should never speak ill of the dead,' said Julia, 'and so I'd better get a move on. I've always thought that Nicholas Pratt was perfectly ghastly. I'm not a particular friend of Amanda's, but he seems to have ruined his daughter's life. Of course you'd know more about that than I do.'

Johnny had no trouble staying silent.

'Why don't you stop being so horrible?' said Robert passionately. 'He's an old man who's really ill and he might hear what you're saying, and he can't even answer back.'

'Yes,' said Thomas, 'it's not fair because he can't answer back.'

Julia at first seemed more bewildered than annoyed,

and when she finally spoke it was with a wounded sigh.

'Well, you know it's time to leave a party when the children start to mount a joint attack on your moral character.'

'Could you say goodbye to Patrick for me?' she said, kissing Johnny abruptly on both cheeks and ignoring the two boys. 'I can't quite face it after what's happened – to Nicholas, I mean.'

'I hope we didn't make her angry,' said Robert.

'She made herself angry, because it was easier for her than being upset,' said Johnny.

Only seconds after her departure, Julia was forced back into the room by the urgent arrival of the waitress, two ambulance men and an array of equipment.

'Look!' said Thomas. 'An oxygen tank and a stretcher. I wish I could have a go!'

'He's over here,' said the waitress unnecessarily.

Nicholas felt his wrist being lifted. He knew his pulse was being taken. He knew it was too fast, too slow, too weak, too strong, everything wrong. A rip in his heart, a skewer through his chest. He must tell them he was not an organ donor, or they would steal his organs before he was dead. He must stop them! Call

Withers! Tell them to *put a stop to it at once.* He couldn't speak. Not his tongue, they mustn't take his tongue. Without speech, thoughts plough on like a train without tracks, buckling, crashing, ripping everything apart. A man asks him to open his eyes. He opens his eyes. Show them he's still compos mentis, compost mentis, recycled parts. No! Not his brain, not his genitals, not his heart, not fit to transplant, still writhing with self in an alien body. They were shining a light in his eyes, no, not his eyes; please don't take his eyes. So much fear. Without a regiment of words, the barbarians, the burning roofs, the horses' hooves beating down on fragile skulls. He was not himself any more; he was under the hooves. He could not be helpless; he could not be humiliated; it was too late to become somebody he didn't know – the intimate horror of it.

'Don't worry, Nick, I'll be with you in the ambulance,' a voice whispered in his ear.

It was the Irish woman. With him in the ambulance! Gouging his eyes out, fishing around for his kidneys with her nimble fingers, taking a hacksaw out of her spiritual tool box. He wanted to be saved. He wanted his mother; not the one he had actually had, but the real one he had never met. He felt a pair of hands grip his feet and another pair of hands slip around his shoulders. Hung, drawn and quartered: publicly executed for all his crimes. He deserved it. Lord have mercy on his soul. Lord have mercy.

The two ambulance men looked at each other and on a nod lifted both ends of Nicholas at once and placed him on the stretcher they had spread out beside him.

'I'm going with him in the ambulance,' said Annette.

'Thank you,' said Patrick. 'Will you call me from the hospital if there's any news?'

'Surely,' said Annette. 'Oh, it's a terrible shock for you,' she said, giving Patrick an unexpected hug. 'I'd better go.'

'Is that woman going with him?' asked Nancy.

'Yes, isn't it kind of her?'

'But she doesn't even know him. I've known Nicholas for ever. First it's my sister and now it's practically my oldest friend. It's too impossible.'

'Why don't you follow her?' said Patrick.

'There is one thing I could do for him,' said Nancy, with a hint of indignation, as if it was a bit much to expect her to be the only person to show any real consideration. 'Miguel, his poor driver, is waiting outside without the least idea of what's happened. I'll go and break the news to him, and take the car on to the hospital, so it's there if Nicholas needs it.'

Nancy could think of at least three places she might stop on the way. The examination was bound to take ages, in fact Nicholas might already be dead, and it would help to take poor Miguel's mind off the dreadful situation if he drove her around all afternoon. She had no cash for taxis, and her swollen feet were already bulging out of the ruthlessly elegant inside edges of her two-thousand-dollar shoes. People said she was incorrigibly extravagant, but the shoes would have cost two thousand dollars *each*, if she hadn't bought them parsimoniously in a sale. She had no prospect of getting any cash for the rest of the month, punished by her beastly bankers for her 'credit history'. Her credit history, as far as she was concerned, was that Mummy had written a lousy will that allowed her evil stepfather to steal all of Nancy's money. Her heroic response had been to spend as if justice had been done, as if she were restoring the natural order of the world by cheating shopkeepers, landlords, decorators, florists, hairdressers, butchers, jewellers and garage owners, by withholding tips from coat-check girls, and by engineering rows with staff so that she could sack them without pay.

On her monthly trip to the Morgan Guaranty – where Mummy had opened an account for her on her twelfth birthday – she collected fifteen thousand dollars in cash. In her reduced circumstances, the walk to Sixty-ninth Street was a Venus flytrap flushed with colour and shining with adhesive dew. She often arrived home with half her month's money spent; sometimes she counted out the entire sum and, seeming mystified by the missing two or three thousand, managed to walk away with a pink marble obelisk or a painting of a monkey in a velvet jacket, promising to come back that afternoon, marking another black spot in the complex maze of her debt, another detour on her city walks. She always gave her real telephone number, with one digit changed, her real address, one block uptown or downtown, and an entirely false name – obviously. Sometimes she called herself Edith Jonson, or Mary de Valençay, to remind herself that she had nothing to be ashamed of, that there had been a time when she could have bought a whole city block, never mind a bauble in one of its shops.

By the middle of the month she was invariably flat

broke. At that point she fell back on the kindness of her friends. Some had her to stay, some let her add her lunches and her dinners to their tabs at Jimmy's or Le Jardin, and others simply wrote her a large cheque, reflecting that Nancy had barged to the front of the queue again and that the victims of floods, tsunamis and earthquakes would simply have to wait another year. Sometimes she created a crisis that forced her trustees to release more capital in order to keep her out of prison, driving her income inexorably lower. For Eleanor's funeral, she was staying with her great friends the Tescos, in their divine apartment in Belgrave Square, a lateral conversion across five buildings on two floors. Harry Tesco had already paid for her air ticket – first class – but she was going to have to break down sobbing in Cynthia's little sitting room before going to the opera tonight, and tell her the terrible pressure she was under. The Tescos were as rich as God and it really made Nancy quite angry that she had to do anything so humiliating to get more money out of them.

'You couldn't drop me off on the way, could you?' Kettle asked Nancy.

'It's Nicholas's private car, dear, not a limo service,'

said Nancy, appalled by the indecency of the suggestion. 'It's really too upsetting when he's so ill.'

Nancy kissed Patrick and Mary goodbye and hurried away.

'It's St Thomas' Hospital, by the way,' Patrick
called after her. 'The ambulance man told me it's the
best place for "clot-busters".'

'Has he had a stroke?' asked Nancy.

'Heart attack, they could tell from the cold nose –
the extremities go cold.'

'Oh, don't,' said Nancy, 'I can't bear to think about
it.'

She set off down the stairs with no time to waste:
Cynthia had made her an appointment at the hairdresser's using the magic words, 'charge it to me'.

When Nancy had left, Henry offered the aggrieved
Kettle a lift. After only a few minutes of complaint
about the rudeness of Patrick's aunt, she accepted, and
said goodbye to Mary and the children. Henry promised to call Patrick the next day, and accompanied
Kettle downstairs. To their surprise they found Nancy
still standing on the pavement outside the club.

'Oh, Cabbage,' she said with a wail of childish
frustration, 'Nicholas's car has gone.'

'You can come with us,' said Henry simply.

Kettle and Nancy sat in the back of the car in hostile silence. Up in front Henry told the driver to go to Princes Gate first, then on to St Thomas' Hospital and finally back to the hotel. Nancy suddenly realized what she had done by accepting a ride. She had forgotten about Nicholas altogether. Now she was going to have to borrow money from Henry to catch a taxi back to the hairdresser's from some godforsaken hospital in the middle of nowhere. It was enough to make you scream.

Nicholas's fall, the commotion that followed, the arrival of the ambulance men and the dispersal of some of the guests had all eluded Erasmus's attention. When Fleur had burst into song in the middle of her conversation with Nicholas, the words 're-clothe us in our rightful minds' sent a little shock through him, like a piercing dog whistle, inaudible to the others but pitched perfectly for his own preoccupations, it recalled him to his true master, insisting that he leave the muddy fields of inter-subjectivity and the intriguing traces of other minds for the cool ledge of the balcony where he might be allowed, for a few moments, to think about thinking. Social life had a tendency to

press him up against his basic rejection of the prop-
osition that an individual identity was defined by
turning experience into an ever more patterned and
coherent story. It was in reflection and not in narrative
that he found authenticity. The pressure to render his
past in anecdote, or indeed to imagine the future in
terms of passionate aspirations, made him feel clumsy
and false. He knew that his inability to be excited by
the memory of his first day at school, or to project a
cumulative and increasingly solid self that wanted to
learn the harpsichord, or longed to live in the Chil-
terns, or hoped to see Christ's blood streaming in the
firmament, made his personality seem unreal to other
people, but it was precisely the unreality of the personality that was so clear to him. His authentic self
was the attentive witness to a variety of inconstant
impressions that could not, in themselves, enhance or
detract from his sense of identity.

Not only did he have an ontological problem with
the generally unquestioned narrative assumptions of
ordinary social life but he also, at this particular party,
found himself questioning the ethical assumption,
shared by everyone except Annette (and not shared
by Annette for reasons that were in themselves prob-
lematic), that Eleanor Melrose had been wrong to

disinherit her son. Setting aside for a moment the difficulties of judging the usefulness of the Foundation she had endowed, there was an undeniable potential Utilitarian merit to the wider distribution of her resources. Mrs. Melrose might at least count on John Stuart Mill and Jeremy Bentham and Peter Singer and R. M. Hare to look sympathetically on her case. If a thousand people, over the years, emerged from the Foundation having discovered, by whatever esoteric means, a sense of purpose that made them into more altruistic and conscientious citizens, would the benefit to society not outweigh the distress caused to a family of four people (with one barely conscious of the loss) who had expected to own a house and turned out not to? In the maelstrom of perspectives could a sound moral judgment be made from any other point of view but that of the strictest impartiality? Whether such a point of view could ever be established was another question to which the answer was almost certainly negative. Nevertheless, even if Utilitarian arithmetic, based on the notion of an unobtainable impartiality, were set aside on the grounds that motivation was desire-based, as Hume had argued, the autonomy of an individual's preferences for one kind of good over another still offered a strong ethical case for Eleanor's philanthropic choice.

There had been a widespread sense of relief when Fleur accompanied Nicholas's stretcher downstairs and appeared to have left the party, but ten minutes later she reappeared resolutely in the doorway. Seeing Erasmus leaning on the balustrade staring pensively down at the gravel path, she immediately expressed her alarm to Patrick.

'What's that man doing on the balcony?' she asked sharply, like a nanny who despairs of leaving the nursery for even a few minutes. 'Is he going to jump?'

'I don't think he was planning to,' said Patrick, 'but I'm sure you could persuade him.'

'The last thing we need is another death on our hands,' said Fleur.

'I'll go and check,' said Robert.

'Me too,' said Thomas, dashing through the French windows.

'You mustn't jump,' he explained, 'because the last thing we need is another death on our hands.'

'I wasn't thinking of jumping,' said Erasmus.

'What were you thinking about?' asked Robert.

'Whether doing some good to a lot of people is

better than doing a lot of good to a few,' Erasmus replied.

'The needs of the many outweigh the needs of the few. Or the one,' said Robert solemnly, making a strange gesture with his right hand.

Thomas, recognizing the allusion to the Vulcan logic of *Star Trek II*, made the same gesture with his hand.

'Live long and prosper,' he said, smiling uncontrollably at the thought of growing pointed ears.

Fleur strode onto the balcony and addressed Erasmus without any trivial preliminaries.

'Have you tried Amitriptyline?' she asked.

'I've never heard of him,' said Erasmus. 'What's he written?'

Fleur realized that Erasmus was much more confused than she had originally imagined.

'You'd better come inside,' she said coaxingly.

Glancing into the room Erasmus noticed that the majority of the guests had left and assumed that Fleur was hinting tactfully that he should be on his way.

'Yes, you're probably right,' said Erasmus.

Fleur reflected that she had a real talent for dealing with people in extreme mental states and that she should probably be put in charge of the depression wing of a psychiatric hospital, or indeed of a national policy unit.

As he went indoors, Erasmus decided not to get entangled in more incoherent social life, but simply to say goodbye to Mary and then leave immediately. As he leant over to kiss her, he wondered if a person of the predominantly narrative type would desire Mary because he had desired her in the past, and whether he would be imagining that fragment of the past being transported, as it were, in a time machine to the present moment. This fantasy reminded him of Wittgenstein's seminal remark that 'nothing is more important in teaching us to understand the concepts we have than constructing fictitious ones'. In his own case, his desire, such as it was, had the character of an inconsequential present-tense fact, like the scent of a flower.

'Thank you for coming,' said Mary.

'Not at all,' mumbled Erasmus, and after squeezing Mary's shoulder lightly, he left without saying goodbye to anyone else.

'Don't worry,' said Fleur to Patrick, 'I'll follow him at a discreet distance.'

'You're his guardian angel,' said Patrick, struggling to disguise his relief at getting rid of Fleur so easily.

Mary followed Fleur politely onto the landing.

'I haven't got time to chat,' said Fleur, 'that poor man's life is in danger.'

Mary knew better than to contradict a woman of Fleur's strong convictions. 'Well, it's been a pleasure to meet such an old friend of Eleanor's.'

'I'm sure she's guiding me,' said Fleur. 'I can feel the connection. She was a saint; she'll show me how to help him.'

'Oh, good,' said Mary.

'God bless you,' Fleur called out as she set off down the stairs at a cracking pace, determined not to lose track of Erasmus's suicidal progress through the streets of London.

'What a woman!' said Johnny, watching through the doorway as Fleur left. 'I can't help feeling that somebody should be following her rather than the other way round.'

'Count me out,' said Patrick, 'I've had an overdose of Fleur. It's a wonder she was ever allowed out of the Priory.'

'She looks to me as if she's just at the beginning of a manic episode,' said Johnny. 'I imagine she was enjoying it too much and decided not to take her pills.'

'Well, let's hope she changes her mind before she

"saves" Erasmus,' said Patrick. 'He might not survive if she rugby tackles him on a bridge, or leaps on him while he's trying to cross the road.'

'God!' said Mary, laughing with relief and amazement. 'I wasn't sure she was ever going to leave. I hope Erasmus made it round the corner before she got outside.'

'I'm going to have to leave myself,' said Johnny. 'I've got a patient at four o'clock.'

He said goodbye to everyone, kissing Mary, hugging the boys, and promising to call Patrick later.

Suddenly the family was alone, apart from the waitress, who was clearing up the glasses and putting the unopened bottles back into a cardboard box in the corner.

Patrick felt a familiar combination of intimacy and desolation, being together and knowing they were about to part.

'Are you coming back with us?' asked Thomas.

'No,' said Patrick, 'I have to go and work.'

'Please,' said Thomas, 'I want you to tell me a story like you used to.'

'I'll see you at the weekend,' said Patrick.

Robert stood by, knowing more than his brother but not enough to understand.

'You can come and have dinner with us if you like,' said Mary.

Patrick wanted to accept and wanted to refuse, wanted to be alone and wanted company, wanted to be close to Mary and to get away from her, wanted the lovely waitress to think that he led an independent life and wanted his children to feel that they were part of a harmonious family.

'I think I'll just . . . crash out,' he said, buried under the debris of contradictions and doomed to regret any choice he made. 'It's been a long day.'

'Don't worry if you change your mind,' said Mary.

'In fact,' said Thomas, 'you should change your mind, because that's what it's for!'

14

As he laboured up to his bedsit, a miniature roof conversion with sloping walls on the fifth floor of a narrow Victorian building in Kensington, Patrick seemed to regress through evolutionary history, growing more stooped with each flight, until he was resting his knuckles on the carpet of the top landing, like an early hominid that has not yet learned to stand upright on the grasslands of Africa and only makes rare and nervous expeditions down from the safety of the trees.

'Fuck,' he muttered, as he got his breath back and raised himself to the level of the keyhole.

It was out of the question to invite that adorable waitress back to his hovel, although her telephone number was nestling in his pocket, next to his disturbingly thumping heart. She was too young to have to squeeze herself out from under the corpse of a middle-aged man who had died in the midst of trying to justify her wearisome climb to his inadequate flat. Patrick collapsed onto the bed and embraced a pillow, imagining its tired feathers and yellowing pillowcase transformed into her smooth warm neck. The anxious aphrodisiac of a recent death; the long gallery of substitutes substituting for substitutes; the tantalizing thirst for consolation: it was all so familiar, but he reminded himself grimly that he had come back to his non-home, now that he was alone at last, in order to be unconsoled. This flat, the bachelor pad of a non-bachelor, the student digs of a non-student, was as good a place as he could wish for to practise being unconsoled. The lifelong tension between dependency and independence, between home and adventure, could be resolved only by being at home everywhere, by learning to cast an equal gaze on the raging self-importance of each mood and incident. He had some way to go. He only had to run out of his favourite bath oil to feel like taking a sledgehammer to the bath and begging a doctor for a Valium script.

Nevertheless, he lay on the bed and thought about how determined he was: a Tomahawk whistling through the woods and thudding into its target, a flash of nuclear light dissolving a circle of cloud for miles around. With a groan he rolled slowly off the bed and sank into the black armchair next to the fireplace. Through the window on the other side of the flat he could see slate roofs sloping down the hill, the spinning metal chimney vents glinting in the late-afternoon sun and, in the distance, the trees in Holland Park, their leaves still too tight-fisted to make their branches green. Before he rang the waitress – he took out the note and found that she was called Helene – before he rang Mary, before he went out for a long sedative dinner and tried to read a serious book, under the dim lighting and over the maddening music, before he pretended that he thought it was important to keep up with current affairs and switched on the news, before he rented a violent movie, or jerked off in the bath because he couldn't face ringing Helene after all, he was going to sit in this chair for a while and show a little respect for the pressures and intimations of the day.

What exactly had he been mourning? Not his mother's death – that was mainly a relief. Not her life – he had mourned her suffering and frustration years ago when she started her decline into dementia. Nor was it his relationship with her, which he had long regarded as an effect on his personality rather than a transaction with another person. The pressure he had felt today was something like the presence of infancy, something far deeper and more helpless than his murderous relationship with his father. Although his father had been there with his rages and his scalpels, and his mother had been there with her exhaustion and her gin, this experience could not be described as a narrative or a set of relationships, but existed as a deep core of inarticulacy. For a man who had tried to talk his way out of everything he had thought and felt, it was shocking to find that there was something huge that he had failed to mention at all. Perhaps this was what he really had in common with his mother, a core of inarticulacy, magnified in her case by illness, but in his case hidden until he heard the news of her death. It was like a collision in the dark in a strange room; he was groping his way round something he couldn't remember being there when the lights went out. Mourning was not the word for this experience. He felt frightened but also excited. In the post-parental realm perhaps he could understand his conditioning as a single fact, without any further interest in its genealogy, not because the historical perspective was untrue, but because it had been renounced. Someone else might achieve this kind of truce before their parents died, but his own parents had been such enormous obstructions that he had to be rid of them in the most literal sense before he could imagine his personality becoming the transparent medium he longed for it to be.

The idea of a voluntary life had always struck him as extravagant. Everything was conditioned by what had gone before; even his fanatical desire for some margin of freedom was conditioned by the drastic absence of freedom in his early life. Perhaps only a kind of bastard freedom was available: in the acceptance of the inevitable unfolding of cause and effect there was at least a freedom from delusion. The truth was that he didn't really know. In any case he had to start by recognizing the degree of his unfreedom, anchored in this inarticulate core that he was now at last embracing, and look on it with a kind of charitable horror. Most of his time had been spent in reaction to his conditioning, leaving little room to respond to the rest of life. What would it be like to react to nothing and respond to everything? He might at least inch in that direction. As he had been trying to tell an unreceptive Julia, he was less persuaded than ever by final judgements or conclusions. He had long suffered from Negative Incapability, the opposite of that famous

Keatsian virtue of being in mysteries, uncertainties and doubts without reaching out for facts and explanations – or whatever the exact phrase was – but now he was ready to stay open to questions that could not necessarily be answered, rather than rush to answers that he refused to question. Maybe he could respond to everything only if he experienced the world as a question, and perhaps he continually reacted to it because he thought that its nature was fixed.

The phone on the little table next to him started to ring and Patrick, dragged out of his thoughts, stared at it for a while as if he had never seen one before. He hesitated and then finally picked it up just before his answerphone message cut in.

'Hello,' he said wearily.

'It's me, Annette.'

'Oh, hi. How are you? How's Nicholas?'

'I'm afraid I've got terrible news,' said Annette. 'Nicholas didn't make it. I'm so sorry, Patrick, I know he was an old family friend. He actually stopped breathing in the ambulance. They tried to revive him when we got to the hospital, but they couldn't get him back. I think all those electrodes and adrenalin are so frightening. When a soul is ready to go, we should let it go gently.'

'It's difficult to find a legal formulation for that approach,' said Patrick. 'Doctors have to pretend that they think more life is always worth having.'

'I suppose you're right, legally,' sighed Annette. 'Anyway, it must be overwhelming for you, and on the day of your mother's funeral.'

'I hadn't seen Nicholas for years,' said Patrick. 'I suppose I was lucky to get a last glimpse of him when he was on top form.'

'Oh, he was an amazing man,' said Annette. 'I've never met anyone quite like him.'

'He was unique,' said Patrick, 'at least I hope so. It would be rather terrifying to find a village full of Nicholas Pratts. Anyhow, Annette,' Patrick went on, realizing that his tone was not quite right for the occasion, 'it was very good of you to go with him. He was lucky to be with someone spontaneously kind at the time of his death.'

'Oh, now you're making me cry,' said Annette.

'And thank you for what you said at the funeral. You reminded me that Eleanor was a good person as well as an imperfect mother. It's very helpful to see her from other points of view than the one I've been trapped in.'

'You're welcome. You know that I loved her.'

'I do. Thank you,' said Patrick again.

They ended the conversation with the improbable promise to talk soon. Annette was flying back to France the next day and Patrick was certainly not going to call her in Saint-Nazaire. Nevertheless he said goodbye with a strange fondness. Did he really think that Eleanor was a good person? He felt that she had made the question of what it meant to be good central – and for that he was grateful.

Patrick took in the news that Nicholas was dead. He pictured him, back in the sixties, in a Mr. Fish shirt, making venomous conversation under the plane trees in Saint-Nazaire. He imagined himself as the little boy he had been at that time, shattered and mad at heart, but with a ferocious, heroic persona, which had eventually stopped his father's abuses with a single determined refusal. He knew that if he was going to understand the chaos that was invading him, he would have to renounce the protection of that fragile hero, just as he had to renounce the illusion of his mother's protection by acknowledging that his parents had been collaborators as well as antagonists.

Patrick sank deeper into the armchair, wondering how much of all this he could stand. Just how unconsoled was he prepared to be? He covered his stomach with a cushion as if he expected to get hit. He wanted to leave, to drink, to dive out of the window into a pool made of his own blood, to cease to feel anything for ever straight away, but he mastered his panic enough to sit back up and let the cushion drop to the floor.

Perhaps whatever he thought he couldn't stand was made up partly or entirely of the thought that he couldn't stand it. He didn't really know, but he had to find out, and so he opened himself up to the feeling of utter helplessness and incoherence that he supposed he had spent his life trying to avoid, and waited for it to dismember him. What happened was not what he had expected. Instead of feeling the helplessness, he felt the helplessness and compassion for the helplessness at the same time. One followed the other swiftly, just as a hand reaches out instinctively to rub a hit shin, or relieve an aching shoulder. He was after all not an infant, but a man experiencing the chaos of infancy welling up in his conscious mind. As the compassion expanded he saw himself on equal terms with his supposed persecutors, saw his parents, who appeared to be the cause of his suffering, as unhappy children with parents who appeared to be the cause of their suffering: there was no one to blame and everyone to help, and those who appeared to deserve the most blame needed the most help. For a while he stayed level with the pure inevitability of things being as they were, the ground zero of events on which skyscrapers of psychological experience were built, and as he imagined not taking his life so personally, the heavy impenetrable darkness of the inarticulacy turned into a silence that was perfectly transparent, and he saw that there was a margin of freedom, a suspension of reaction, in that clarity.

Patrick slid back down in his chair and sprawled in front of the view. He noticed how his tears cooled as they ran down his cheeks. Washed eyes and a tired and empty feeling. Was that what people meant by peaceful? There must be more to it than that, but he didn't claim to be an expert. He suddenly wanted to see his children, real children, not the ghosts of their ancestors' childhoods, real children with a reasonable chance of enjoying their lives. He picked up the phone and dialled Mary's number. He was going to change his mind. After all, that's what Thomas said it was for.